# ALL FOR GOOD

ROSEANN MCGRATH BROOKS

D1715149

ALL FOR GOOD

*To Truman and Mom and Dad, for everything.*

# PROLOGUE

## OUTER BANKS, NORTH CAROLINA

21 Years Ago

"Why can't I go with you, Danny?" Emily crossed her arms and stomped her tiny bare foot on the sand.

Danny took a deep breath of the sharp, salty air and then, with his bottom lip curled up, blew out an exasperated sigh that ruffled his sun-streaked bangs.

"Because you're too little," he explained with exaggerated patience. "You're not even in kindergarten yet." It was only Tuesday of vacation week, and Emily was already bugging him to death.

"But *you're* going!"

"The big kids said I could go this time," Danny argued. "I'm starting third grade soon." Nathan, Abby, Aaron, and even his own brother Matthew—the coolest of the older kids, Danny thought—had finally agreed that he could hang out with all of them. Of course, hanging out simply meant walking two blocks along the waterline to the jetty, but it was an exciting adventure, and it implied that he had been accepted into the fun gang.

"You can stay with Lauren." Danny turned to follow the others, who had already begun walking ahead.

"She's a baby," Emily grumbled, and Daniel cringed as he heard her sprinting to catch up with him, sloshing through the shallow water splashing against the shore.

~

"Emmy, come back to the blankets," Emily's father called. She turned around and glared at her dad—but was smart enough not to talk back.

"Honey, when you get bigger, you can hike with them." Her father reached where she had been standing and grabbed her hand to walk them both back to where the adults were sitting in chairs and on towels on the beach. "Maybe next year. For now, stay with the rest of us. Paige is here, and the Kochkas and Delanceys are coming down any minute now."

Emily huffed. The other kids were OK. But they weren't awesome like Danny.

# CHAPTER ONE

## THE POCONOS MOUNTAINS, PENNSYLVANIA

Present Day

E mily let out a long breath and rolled her neck in a slow circle, listening to the crinkling sounds it made. In her pocket, her cell phone vibrated against her hip, reminding her it was midnight.

"I've got to get some sleep." She smiled weakly at Brandon as she gathered up her purse and jacket from underneath the welcome desk of the inn. It had been a sunny end-of-the-summer day when she had left her apartment that morning, but it would be cool now. "I have to be back again tomorrow morning at 8!"

Brandon put his arm around her waist and leaned in to kiss her, but they both jumped when the automatic double doors swished open. Emily breathed a small sigh of relief. She and Brandon had been dating for about two months, and he always seemed to be pushing things to move a little faster than she'd like.

A tall, lean man in a dark-grey suit that was clearly custom made walked through the entranceway wheeling a small black suitcase behind him. He had a black laptop case slung over one shoulder and was texting as he moved. His head was down, which meant that his short, carefully combed, light-brown hair was all Emily could see. Curious, she stood off to the side as Brandon stepped forward to the edge of the front counter to greet their guest.

The man was still texting, so Brandon waited patiently. The guest grunted at his phone and then looked up.

"Sorry," the man said. "Daniel Caine."

Emily gasped, and Daniel looked to where she was standing. She dropped her purse, ran to him, and threw her arms around her old friend.

"Danny!" she exclaimed, pulling back from her hug. "What are you doing here?"

"Emmy Steverman?" Daniel's eyebrows rose. "Hey, I can't believe you're still here at the inn! I'm really late." He shoved his phone into his front pants pocket. "I called ahead to ask when you were working, and I was going to surprise you. But I thought your shift was over at 7, and I got super held up at work. I figured I'd missed you."

"I stayed an extra few hours to fill in for a woman who called in sick," Emily explained. "How did you even know I worked here?"

Daniel grinned. "C'mon. My folks get your folks' Christmas cards. The last one said you were working at a Pocono inn. I have a conference in Mount Pocono this week, and I didn't feel like staying in the conference hotel." He shrugged. "I called your mom, and she gave me the name of this place. And here I am at good old Sweet Fern Inn." His smile grew mischievous. "But really, is there actually such a thing as a sweet fern?"

"Oh, my gosh, it's amazing to see you," Emily gushed. "It's been, what, four years? And yes, smarty pants, those lovely green ferns all along this street are sweet ferns. You probably couldn't see them in the dark." She tried to stifle a yawn.

"Hey, if you've been here since this morning, you need to get to bed," Daniel said. "I do too. Long day tomorrow. But can we catch up for dinner maybe tomorrow night?"

"Sounds great." Emily nodded and acknowledged the exhaustion hitting her. "We can eat here. Our inn's restaurant is fantastic; just let me know what time you'd like to meet. I don't live far, so I can go home after my shift and then come back to meet you whenever you'd like. I have off the next day."

"It's a date," Daniel declared, continuing to grin.

"Ahem."

Daniel and Emily looked over to see Brandon scowling at them.

"Oh, Danny, this is my friend Brandon," Emily explained. Brandon cleared his throat again. Emily smiled, unfazed. "I mean, my boyfriend."

Daniel put out his hand. "Hi, I'm Daniel." Then he gently punched Emily's upper arm. He looked surprised. "Hey, your arm is almost level with mine. You're all grown up."

Emily rolled her eyes dramatically as Daniel looked back toward Brandon. "Anyway," Daniel continued, ignoring her, "this squirt and I go way back."

"Remember when I told you about the four families that would vacation together in the Outer Banks every year?" Emily asked Brandon. "The dads were all fraternity brothers? Well, Danny is one of the other nine kids!"

"And Emmy is *the* one of the other nine who used to drive me crazy!" Danny teased, and he leaned down to gently bump his shoulder against hers.

Emily yawned again but still managed to lightly slap Daniel's arm in return. "I gotta sleep," she announced. "I'll see you tomorrow, Danny." She lowered her voice in mock seriousness. "I mean, *Daniel.* G'night, Brandon." She gave her boyfriend a light kiss on his cheek.

After Emily left, Daniel finished checking in and headed to the elevators. He smiled to himself as he waited. Brandon clearly was not pleased at Daniel's arrival. If Brandon only knew he had nothing to worry about! Emily was kind of like family. Well, not family exactly, but a really close friend. For goodness' sake, she was years younger than Daniel was.

As he stepped into the elevator and pushed the button for floor 4, the top floor, Daniel rethought that. Well, she actually wasn't that much younger than he was. What *was* the age difference? Three years? He'd dated women younger than she was. But this was little Emmy.

He smiled at the memories that streamed through his mind. He, Emmy, and the other kids were always having "adventures," as they called them, and he remembered the pure and simple joy of those summers.

Only now, little Emmy was an adult woman. That long, straight blonde hair that used to stick up in all directions was cropped fashionably to brush her shoulders. As a kid, he had always viewed Emmy as tall and skinny, nearly gawky. Now she looked graceful, like a dancer. Her voice had mellowed. Her eyes were the same, however: clear blue eyes that told you exactly what she was feeling and gently penetrated your defenses to decipher what you were feeling. At least, that's the way it was when they were kids.

As he headed down the hall to his room, he suddenly remembered John 1:47: "Here is truly an Israelite in whom there is no deceit." OK, that passage was about the disciple Nathaniel, and Emily wasn't anything like Nathanael in the Bible, but she really was a person with no deceit, no guile. In his line of work as a financial advisor, when was the last time he could say that about anyone?

The old hotel, with that quaint name of Sweet Fern Inn, still used metal keys instead of digital key cards, and he pulled the jangling hardware out of his pocket. He liked the click it made as he turned it. He pushed open the old carved-pine door and nearly sighed out loud. The first thing he noticed was the imposing four-poster bed with thick oak spindles that was covered in a quilt with squares of dark-brown and light-blue patterns. It was flanked by two oak end tables. A light-brown, high-backed armchair sat in one corner. Across from the bed was the nod to modernism. A flat-screen TV was mounted above a basic rectangular particle-board hotel bureau with three long drawers. Next to that stood a simple brown desk that was topped with a desk lamp and a power strip and accompanied by a black swivel chair from an office supply store.

Dried flowers or bark or some sort of plant pieces rested in a medium-sized wooden bowl on the desk, the potpourri emitting a light cinnamon scent. Between the sweet, spicy smell and the big bed calling to him, Daniel ignored his buzzing cell phone, tossing it on the bureau, and instead turned down the covers. When the phone stopped, he realized that its zizzing had been the only noise in the room. This time, he did sigh out loud. Then he slipped out of his suit, threw his clothes on the floor, pulled on a T-shirt and gym shorts that he had taken out of his suitcase, and fell asleep in five minutes.

# CHAPTER TWO

Emily took a nap after work the next day in order to be refreshed for dinner. As she put on her tan pants and a flowing navy-blue and tan blouse, she thought about how much she was looking forward to catching up with her friend. Even though they had spent only one week a year together on vacation while growing up, those shore memories were among her favorites.

Emily's and Daniel's dads, as well as the two other fathers on those North Carolina vacations, had been in a service fraternity together in college. The four men had begun their joint annual Outer Banks vacation before any of them were married, but the trips continued for several decades after the fraternity brothers added wives and children to the group. As a result, the children of the four families grew up together—at least for that one week every summer. Because Emily was toward the end of the babies born—there were eventually ten of them—she was in her teens when different members of different families started missing the vacation week because of college or new jobs. By the time she was 16, they had stopped going to the Outer Banks all together—although they regrouped again for one last hurrah the summer of her 22$^{nd}$ birthday.

Danny was in the middle of the pack of kids, closer in age to

Emily's brother and sister, the twins Aaron and Abby, but it was Danny that Emily had always tried to keep up with during their vacations. He always seemed to have the most creative hiding spots and the best ideas for games. She knew she had been a pest to him and a few of the others when she was little, but when they reunited four years ago in Corolla, North Carolina, the difference in the children's ages had blurred, and they were on equal footing. That had been an extra-special week. They were once again like one big happy family.

Except, of course, for Paige. Emily felt the familiar stab of pain, and she shook her head. She missed her big sister every day, but she wouldn't let those feelings dim her excitement about tonight's dinner. She could practically feel Paige mussing her hair and hear her saying, "Hey, silly girl, don't feel sad about me. Have a fun time with crazy Danny."

Danny—*Daniel*, she corrected herself as she walked—was already seated in the restaurant when Emily arrived. He stood up when she got to the small square table and moved around to pull out the chair across from him. That gallantry made her giggle. He frowned.

"What?"

"We're really grown up," Emily contended. "Fifteen years ago, you would have pulled that chair out far enough for me to fall!"

Daniel laughed. "It does feel kind of weird and out of context. For one thing, I don't think I've ever seen you in anything but shorts or a bathing suit!"

It was Emily's turn to laugh as she opened up her menu, taking note that the waiter had already placed water on the table for both of them.

"You look lovely, by the way," Daniel added.

"Thanks." Emily could feel herself blushing, and she lifted the two-page menu slightly to hide her face. "Well, how was your conference today?" she asked, pretending to focus on her meal choice. She gave that up quickly and closed the pages to look at her friend. Daniel was still in business attire. He wore the same suit he had on the night before but with a different shirt. Tonight, he had ditched the tie and unbuttoned the collar of his light-blue Oxford, which made his dark blue eyes seem even more intense.

Those eyes narrowed, and Daniel groaned. "Oh, you have no idea how tedious these things are. And I'm expected to be 'on' all day long. I have to be nice to everyone because they could end up being a client or a partner one day. That's one of the reasons I came to the inn. It made it easier to avoid the after-conference drinks and socializing."

Daniel waved his hand in front of his chest as if to swipe away the activities of his conference. "Enough about my day. And what have you been doing since you finished college?"

"That's right," Emily said, placing her menu back on the table. "I had just graduated that summer of our last Outer Banks reunion."

Daniel grew serious. "Emily, I'm really sorry about Paige. I know we all got together there to remember her that year and spread her ashes, but I never got to truly say I'm sorry about her death."

Emily lowered her head for a moment, but when she lifted it, she made sure she was smiling, even if it was a wistful smile. "Thanks. Our whole family had been in shock since Paige's accident in March that year, and my folks really wanted a way to remember the good times. That trip was a great way to do that. This may sound corny, but it was very healing."

"How did you manage to get through that last semester at school?" Daniel asked. Before Emily could answer, his next words rushed out. "I'm sorry. You probably don't want to talk about it."

"No, that's fine." Emily ran her index finger along the cool side of the water glass, watching the condensation slide toward the table. "In some ways, I almost don't remember that last semester. I went to a small college, and all the professors knew me and were very support-ive. I had had good grades up until then. I think several of them let me slide a little."

They stopped their conversation as the waiter arrived to take their order.

"Hey, Em," the waiter said, clearly surprised to see her there. "This man said he was expecting another person when I brought the water, but I didn't know it would be you!"

"Hi, Mike," Emily greeted him back. "This is my old friend Daniel."

"You don't look that old," Mike joked.

"He's known me since before I was born," Emily said. "He really *is* old!"

Mike tilted his head in question.

"His family spent vacations with my family," Emily explained. "That means my mom was pregnant with me when he was three."

Daniel chuckled. "Like I remember that."

They placed their orders, and Mike retreated to the kitchen.

"Anyway," Emily said, continuing where they left off, "I had the most amazing support network from our Christian fellowship at school. Those friends got me through that spring. They helped me realize that Jesus was weeping *with* me at the loss of Paige. They prayed for me when I couldn't pray anymore. It helped me get over the anger. I still keep in contact with a lot of those friends."

Daniel shifted in his chair. "Well, that's nice."

Emily sat up straighter and grinned. "Then I graduated with a hospitality management degree and got this great gig at a historic Pocono hotel. There's a rumor that Jackie Gleason played golf here!"

"Cool." Daniel seemed to appreciate the change of subject. "Do you always work the front desk?"

"Not always," Emily responded. "I also do a number of business-related things in sales. Sometimes, I work with the event team on weddings and birthday parties and stuff. I really like doing that, and the owners let me do as much of that as they can. It's just that front-desk help can be hard to find. We're trying to partner with a local university to offer paid internships. Maybe if kids are getting both money and a grade, they'll be more responsible coming to work!"

When their salads arrived, Emily paused and bowed her head. Because of Daniel's earlier discomfort when she mentioned prayer, she didn't make a big deal about what she was doing but she knew he'd recognize that she was praying. She finished in less than a minute, lifted her head, and smiled. "Dig in," she advised. "Jim makes the best homemade balsamic vinaigrette."

# CHAPTER THREE

E mily was right: the salad was terrific, with just the right combination of sweet and tangy in the dressing. They finished their first course in comfortable silence. When the waiter delivered Daniel's chicken Marsala, mushrooms and wine sauce were nearly spilling off his plate. His mouth dropped.

Emily smiled. "See, I told you this restaurant is great. It's not just the amount of food, either; it's good food." Emily cut off a piece of her own salmon.

"This inn is quite a find," Daniel agreed, trying to determine the best way to attack his meal. "It was pitch black outside last night, but I had left my curtains open to let the sun in for this morning. And when I woke up—wow. The view is incredible."

"You must have a back room!" Emily nearly squealed. "That's great! You're looking at the mountain for Winter Wonderland Ski Slope."

"Get out! Oh, I am definitely bringing my skiing buddies up here this winter."

"Make your reservations now," Emily advised. "We only have 40 rooms, 10 on each floor, and this place books up in ski season."

They each ate more of their main courses before Emily spoke

again. "Now *you* know what *I* do for a living. What's up with you in the world of finance?"

Daniel was already getting full, so he put down his fork. "Well, it certainly doesn't have the beauty you have here. Plus, I'm sure I don't see the variety of clients that you do! But I like my job a lot. And I feel as if I'm good at it. It's a lot of work, but it's the right fit for me for now. And I like being smack dab in center-city Philly."

"And what about a girlfriend?" Emily asked. "I think you had just started seeing someone when I last caught up with you a few years ago. Is that still going strong?"

Daniel cringed and then smiled. "I don't even remember who that might have been. "I've had a couple of short-term relationships, but I tend to be a bit of a workaholic, and consequently, women don't stick around too long. I do like to think I'm a romantic, though. I'll know it when I see it."

"It?"

"Her." Daniel laughed apologetically. "You know what I mean. Anyway, what about you and Brandon?"

Now Emily was the one to put down her fork. "We've only been seeing each other a couple of months. I like him. He's confident and ambitious, and he's very friendly. I'm not sure where things are going yet, but that's fine with both of us, I think." She paused. "He's a Christian, and that's important to me. But we go to different churches. That's actually kind of good. It gives us a bunch of meaty things to talk about."

"That's nice." Daniel leaned forward to finish off the rest of his chicken.

He noticed that Emily began to take another attempt at her food as well but then looked up. "Hey," how long are you here for? I was going to check your reservation today, and I forgot."

"My conference is finished on Thursday. I'll check out of here that morning and take my bags to Mount Pocono to the conference with me."

Emily dropped her hands to her lap. "Bummer," she said. "I guess you can't sneak away to go hiking with Brandon and me tomorrow. We're heading to Blakeslee Nature Trail."

"Unfortunately, no. I'm actually giving a presentation in the morning."

"Oh, well." Emily shrugged. "Maybe next time.

They finished their meals, and Mike dropped off the check.

"I can expense this" Daniel pulled the bill toward himself. "I'm allowed enough for me and a 'dinner companion.'"

"Thanks," Emily said. "I loved being your dinner companion. This was so much fun!"

"Hey, I wasn't joking about skiing," Daniel explained as he pulled out his wallet. "A couple of my work buddies and I take a four-day weekend in February every year to ski up this way. I'll make my reservations for us at the inn before I leave."

Emily brightened. "Give me the dates, and maybe I can take a few days off and join you."

Daniel put his hand to his mouth to hide a smile. "Are you sure? As I remember, you weren't the best water skier when we went that time in Corolla Light in the Outer Banks!"

Emily threw her napkin at her friend. "Hey, I was, what, like 10 years old the year we did that."

"Bailey and Abby were teasing you about being too young, and you were furious." Daniel grinned as he remembered. "You always wanted that 'adventure'—even before you could pronounce the word. You used to say, 'I want a babenture,' too. And boy, no one could ever tell you that you were too young for anything! You just strapped on those giant skis and spent most of the ride on your stomach, with your face in the water."

Emily laughed and then faked an air of superiority. "I've matured," she stated, and then admitted, "I never did take to water skiing, but I can hold my own on downhill skis."

Daniel chuckled too. "OK, we'll see. But if Brandon was jealous of *me*, he's going to lose it when I bring my friends. They're all single and 'looking for love.'"

Emily shook her head, but she was still smiling. They both recognized that it was time to leave, and they stood. Emily grabbed Daniel in a tight hug. "I'll see you in a few months," she said.

"Looking forward to it."

Two days later, rather than doing a quick electronic checkout, Daniel went to the lobby to settle up his bill. He was disappointed that it was Brandon and not Emily standing at the front desk, but he tried to be friendly. "Hi again, Brandon," he said. "I'm Emily's friend. I'm checking out."

Emily must have talked with Brandon about her relationship with Daniel, because the other man seemed less threatened and was, if not friendly, at least pleasant. Daniel booked a four-man suite for the first week of the following February and began to walk away when Brandon called him back.

"I forgot that Emily left this note for you," Brandon explained. The icy demeanor was back.

"Thanks."

*Danny, great to see you. Remember Jackson Delancey? He's a principal dancer in NYC Ballet, and we're going to see him in a lead role around Thanksgiving. Wanna join us? – Emmy*

It seemed like a good plan.

# CHAPTER FOUR

Facebook Messenger

September 8, Daniel: *Thanks for friending me, Emily Steverman. I'm not on Facebook that often, but I lurk.*

September 9, Emily: *I'm not on often, either. But I tend to post nerdy photos, especially of Pocono fall foliage.*

September 20, Daniel: *What's up? I thought you were going to post photos. You know, fall foliage and all.*

September 22, Emily: *Patience, patience. It was a warm summer.*

~

Facebook Posts

September 30, Emily: *Four tree photos from the top-floor balcony at the inn. Daniel Caine, these are for you!*

September 30, Daniel: *It's about time!*

September 30, Lauren Caine: *Hi, Emily Steverman. It's me, Daniel's much smarter and much better-looking sister. Your photos are gorgeous.*

October 2, Emily: *Looks like a good year for the trees. You're welcome to come for a visit. You can stay with me. I have a guest bedroom.*

October 2, Lauren: *I have a school break soon. I may take you up on that.*

S eptember had been busier than usual at the firm, and Daniel felt as if he needed a few days off. He had even lost several weekends during which he had to play golf with potential clients. Yes, he enjoyed his job, and yes, in the end it was the right thing to do for business, but having to continually put on a happy face was beginning to wear on him. Plus, he really didn't like golf.

It was Friday night at the gym at the YMCA, and he didn't have any plans for the weekend. He was thrilled. One of his workout buddies, Paul, moved into spotting position behind Daniel, who had laid on his back on a weight bench.

"We're going canoeing on the Brandywine tomorrow," Paul mentioned, standing above Daniel's head. "Wanna come?"

Daniel grunted and then pushed the barbell straight up from his chest. "Sure," he managed to say. "Who's going?"

"Me, Will, and Jose," Paul explained. "I think Jose might be bringing Maddie."

Daniel couldn't speak any more as he finished his reps. He finally stationed the bar and sat up. Then he grabbed a towel from Paul and wiped his face. "Is Maddie the girl Jose met from eHarmony?" Daniel asked.

"Yeah." Paul traded places with his friend. "I've met her once or twice. She seems nice. He really likes her."

"That's great," Daniel said, meaning it. Now that he was in his late twenties—nearly 30, he reminded himself—his friends were gradually beginning to settle down, and he was happy for them. It was at these times of hearing about others being joyfully coupled that he would get a quick pang of something. He wasn't sure what the feeling was, but he thought it might be a little like longing. His parents were happily married, and he knew he didn't want anything less than the blissfulness they seemed to have, despite a few heartaches over the years. He wanted to find someone he could share that bond with, but there never seemed to be time for that. And when he did find the time, there never seemed to be the right person.

He began to wonder if maybe he should put a little more effort into it.

"Uh, a little help here?" Paul said. He had swapped places with Daniel but was still lying on his back and waving his arms in front of Daniel's face. "I'm not lifting if you're not paying attention."

"Oh, sorry," Daniel said. "I was just thinking of Jose and Maddie. And you have Marissa. Maybe I should start looking."

Paul wrapped his fingers around the bar but didn't begin lifting yet. "Dude, you're not going to find the perfect woman if you're a workaholic." Paul pulled the bar off the stand and pushed upward. "You gotta get out more."

Daniel just shook his head and let Paul finish his workout.

When Paul was done, he wiped his face and pointed a towel-draped arm at Daniel. "And you're not going to find her here—not at this testosterone-heavy gym!"

Daniel just rolled his eyes and moved to the mats.

Later, as the two walked to the locker room, Paul asked, "Hey, did your folks ever give your brother that money?"

"The $800 he needed for first month's rent on a new apartment? Yeah."

Paul groaned in sympathy.

"Matthew and Cult-Wife have a new baby," Daniel explained. "That's my folks' second granddaughter. Actually, she's my second niece, too. My parents didn't want that poor new little girl—or her older sister—to be homeless."

"What's Cult-Wife's real name again?" Paul asked.

"Mary Rose." Daniel laughed mirthlessly. "Good Christian name, huh?"

Paul clapped his arm around Daniel, but his tone was sensitive. "They'll get out of that cult someday soon, I'm sure of it. Man, from what you've told me before, Matthew and his wife believe such crazy stuff."

"It's not just the things they believe," Daniel spit out. "If they want to believe crazy stuff, hey, that's on them. But it affects a lot of other people, too, especially my family. Because they don't live in a commune or anything and, on the surface, they look as if they live normal lives, a lot of people don't understand how hard it is. Matthew and Mary Rose won't take part in any family holiday gatherings because they say, for example, that Christmas is a 'pagan' celebration. They won't go to family funerals or weddings or even covered dish dinners because they think regular Christian churches are 'evil.' They go to cult services or studies or work parties so often at night and on weekends that they never get enough sleep, which means they're sick all the time—even the kids. And then they give a boatload of money to the cult leaders and barely have enough for food or diapers."

Daniel appreciated that his friend waited for him to finish. Then Paul put an arm around Daniel's shoulder and said quietly, "There are a lot of people praying for them. They can't stay in that group for much longer."

Daniel nodded, but he wasn't quite as sure. His parents prayed every day for that miracle. They had been praying for five years. He himself had stopped praying when Mary Rose got pregnant last year with his brother's second child. His whole family had hoped the stress of the first child would have squeezed them out of that stupid organization, but now Matthew and his wife had brought another daughter into the creepiness. Daniel figured that after all this time, praying wasn't going to help. He didn't know where God was in all this, but it seemed as if the Almighty wasn't paying attention or just wasn't interested.

Daniel knew his parents were concerned about Daniel's own frustration with God, and he found it ironic that they prayed for him as fervently as they prayed for his brother. Matthew was in a cult; Daniel knew he wasn't nearly as messed up as his brother. And Daniel hadn't broken his parents' heart the way Matthew had. Matthew's cult supposedly believed that Jesus was the Son of God, but they also believed in a whole host of other gods. And their gods told them that they couldn't celebrate Christmas and Easter. Seriously? The birth and resurrection of one of their gods? And what did those other fake gods have against the holidays? And families? It was just dumb—and hurtful.

On occasion, Daniel wondered if the real God was "testing" them all. If so, he figured he was probably failing.

Daniel shook his head as he showered at the Y. He was mad that Paul had brought up Matthew. Daniel liked it way better when he could avoid thinking about his brother. He had mastered the defense mechanism of denial when it came to Matthew and the cult.

As he washed his hair, Daniel tried to focus on the canoe trip tomorrow. That would be fun. He had always been able to get a real sense of peace out in nature.

Just then, he was surprised that Sweet Fern Inn and Emily's photos popped into his head. He had turned one of her shots of a red maple tree with fiery bright crimson and yellow leaves into his screen saver at work. If the Brandywine River trip tomorrow didn't settle him, maybe he'd plan for a long weekend in the Poconos sometime before ski season.

# CHAPTER FIVE

"I found a new place to hike," Brandon called from Emily's living room.

Emily walked out of her bedroom carrying her gym socks and hiking shoes and headed toward her forest-green, fabric couch where Brandon had plopped when he arrived. The couch had been her first grown-up furniture purchase. She had already brought to the apartment a queen-size bed that her parents bought her for college, but she had needed living room furniture. Consequently, she used her first big paycheck to buy this sofa—with memory foam—and matching chair and ottoman. Later, she added a recliner, coffee table, and end tables, but she always felt nostalgic about her original living room set.

Emily sat next to Brandon on the couch and kissed him on the cheek. As she turned to begin putting on her socks, Brandon lightly took her face in his and met her lips with his own. She kissed him back gently but shifted away as he began pulling her closer to him.

Over the past few weeks, Brandon had been getting increasingly insistent with his physical affection. He didn't force anything, but she could tell he was becoming more and more frustrated with her. She knew they probably needed to talk about this, but it was an embarrassing subject. And she had begun to wonder if her lack of enthusiasm ran deeper than simply not wanting a more physical liaison. Brandon was nice, but she had recently been questioning whether or not she truly wanted this to be a long-term relationship.

"Oh, I meant to ask you." Emily tried to steer Brandon away from kissing her again. "You're coming with my friend Suzie and me to see Jackson dance right before Thanksgiving weekend, right?"

"Huh?"

Emily bumped Brandon playfully with her shoulder as she pulled on her second sock. "Remember that I told you that I have a friend in the ballet in New York? Suzie and I are going to see him dance in November, and I'm hoping we can get a bunch of people to go."

Brandon scoffed. "Really? The ballet? A bunch of goofy guys in tights? Yeah, that's not going to happen."

Emily's head jerked up and she turned to stare at Brandon. She was so taken aback by his comment that she wasn't sure how to respond. He shrugged and rubbed the back of his neck.

"Hey, I've got big news." Brandon stood up to avoid Emily's gaze. "I have an interview in Philly next week." He walked over to the island that separated her kitchen from the living room and grabbed a bagel from a basket on the counter. He pulled the dry bagel apart and began eating one half of it.

Brandon had been talking a lot lately about applying for a position at one of the big hotel chains in Philadelphia. He kept saying that he wanted to "leave this one-horse town" and climb the corporate ladder in the hospitality industry. He was trying to convince Emily to do the same.

The thing was, Emily didn't have those ambitions. She was hoping to take on more responsibility at the inn, but she loved the variety of work she was currently doing. She had even talked about contacting the firm that did the wedding coordination for Sweet Fern to see if she could help them more proactively with their events. One of the owners of the inn, Kim Garrett, had already encouraged her to do that. Most important, she didn't want to leave her job or her town. Her friends were here, her church was here, and she loved being able to enjoy the outdoors during the different seasons.

Her boyfriend wanted something else. And she was aware that thinking about said boyfriend moving away did not make her sad.

Brandon put down his bagel and reached over the back of the couch to grab her hand. "This new hiking place is way more secluded," he said, suggestively wiggling his eyebrows. "It's gonna be fun!"

Emily stayed seated. She suddenly realized that she and Brandon were definitely not on the same page in many ways—and that they really didn't belong together as a couple. In fact, she also acknowledged to herself that the realization was not as sudden as she thought it was. However, knowing this meant that what she was doing with Brandon was essentially stringing him along, and that was not fair. She had had a few men do that to her in the course of her dating life, and she didn't like it. Emily enjoyed Brandon's friendship, but that was all. She kept Brandon's hand in hers and gently led him around to sit again on the sofa next to her.

"Brandon, I think we want different things in life," Emily began. Brandon shook his head and looked at her blankly.

"Like you want to go to Philly to the Hilton or Four Seasons, right?" she asked.

He nodded. "I already have an interview on Wednesday, like I told you."

"I like it here," Emily explained.

There was a pause.

"Are you breaking up with me?" Brandon's face colored slightly.

Emily was relieved that Brandon had gotten to the heart of the conversation quickly. "I don't want to hurt you," she said. "I just think we make better friends than boyfriend and girlfriend. In fact, there's that rep from Harris Hotels in the city who stays at the inn once a month—"

"Karen," Brandon interrupted angrily.

"Yeah, Karen. She clearly likes you, and you two have a lot of interests in common: disc golf, antiquing, those sorts of things. And Harris properties are all over the place."

Brandon looked down, his brow furrowed.

"I understand if you're mad at me." Emily lightly placed her hand on his lowered shoulder. "But I'd like to stay friends."

There was another pause, and then Brandon rose abruptly. "I don't think so, Emily." He glared at her. "You're actually too 'holier-than-thou' for me to be friends with."

Emily was shocked—and not a little bit hurt. However, she knew Brandon was angry, and he had every right to be. She stood up. "I'm sorry, Brandon," she said quietly and tried to reach again for his hand.

He twisted away from her grasp and marched to her door. "Yeah," he called as he opened the door. "See you at work." He slammed her door behind him.

Emily sat back down on the couch and stayed there several minutes after Brandon had gone. She knew she had done the right thing, but it still stung. She really did like him, and she would miss his friendship. However, it would have been cruel to keep dating him when she didn't feel that way toward him. Finally, she looked down at her favorite deep-purple hiking shoes, which she had finished lacing up shortly after Brandon had walked out.

"I still want to go hiking," she said aloud. But she needed to be alone to think through the breakup, and it was never safe to go on the trails alone.

But there was always Chloe.

Chloe was a yellow Labrador Retriever owned by Marc and Mara Jenner, an older couple whose house stood next to Emily's apartment complex. She had met them when she first moved in a few years earlier. She had been out walking to get to know the neighborhood, and they were taking their new puppy for her first walk. Chloe had been immediately smitten with Emily, and the feeling was mutual. Thus, whenever the Jenners took their trips across the country to visit their only daughter in San Francisco, the couple asked Emily to house-sit and dog-sit. She loved those bonding times with Chloe.

Emily knocked on the Jenners' door, and Mara answered almost immediately.

"Can Chloe come out and play?" Emily asked. Mara smiled and let Emily in.

"I lost my hiking partner this morning, and Chloe would be a great buddy in the woods," Emily explained. Mara pulled Chloe's leash off the hook by the front door, and the yellow dog barked and then circled the two women in frantic anticipation, tail swishing across Mara's and Emily's legs.

"Put this on her, and I'll go get the plastic bags." Mara maneuvered through Chloe's weaving, left the room, and then called back. "You know it's my pet peeve when dog owners don't clean up—even in the woods."

Emily laughed. "It's hard enough for us hikers to dodge the deer droppings." Chloe barked again.

"I saw Brandon leaving the building in a huff earlier," Mara commented, coming back to the room and handing Emily a few bags from the local Weis grocery store. "I don't mean to pry, but is that why you're on your own today?"

"Yeah," Emily replied somberly. "We've 'agreed to part ways,' as they say. I'm a little sad, but breaking up is the right thing to do." She bent down and ruffled Chloe's head. "I'll tell Chloe all about it on our walk."

# CHAPTER SIX

The following Monday morning, Emily's cell phone dinged, indicating she had received a text. She was in the inn's main business office, sitting at the huge mahogany-finished desk and working on the final touches to the wedding scheduled for the upcoming weekend. She had rolled up the sleeves of her white blouse, which had the green Sweet Fern logo and leaf on the right pocket, and was studying the top page of a pile of papers in front of her. Emily loved assisting with the wedding planning, and she was honored that the Garretts, who owned the inn, appreciated her help coordinating the logistics with the outside agency that handled the event planning. She put her pencil down on her list of "Things to Do: 1 Week Before" and took a quick sip of her homemade mint iced tea before checking her text.

*Emmy, it's Lauren Caine. Did you mean what you said about visiting sometime?*

Emily replied that she most definitely did. Immediately, her phone rang, and it was the same number that had texted her.

"Hi, Emily," Lauren began. "I know it's short notice, but I was really hoping to come this weekend."

"That would be perfect," Emily said. "I'm actually off this weekend. We have a wedding coming up, and I've been working on that pretty intensely the past few weeks. But they bring in a professional wedding coordinator for the big day itself."

Lauren sighed. "Well, I'm still not sure if it's going to work. We had it all planned out. My boyfriend and I wanted to check out the mountains, and my parents were a bit overprotective about the two of us going to the Poconos alone. So my brother Danny said he'd chaperone us. He and Jason—that's my boyfriend—were going to stay at the inn while I stayed at your place, if that was OK with you."

"Sure."

"But the inn is booked!" Lauren said the last word on a long whine.

"Oh, yeah, of course," Emily remembered. "The wedding."

"There are no secret hidden rooms that you save for special guests or anything?" Lauren's voice rose hopefully.

Emily chuckled. "No. But you guys can all still stay at my place if you personally don't mind sharing a bed with me. One of the guys can stay in the spare bedroom, and the other can sleep on the couch."

"Oh, Emmy, really? You'd let us do that?"

Now she sounds like the enthusiastic little girl I remember, Emily thought. "No problem. If you don't mind my tagging along, I know just the place to take you at Delaware Water Gap. Great views. Great photos."

After Lauren effervesced her thanks, and Emily got assurances that no one would have an allergic reaction to her cat, Big Boy, Emily hung up, smiling. She went back to her checklist, and 10 minutes later, her phone dinged again. This time, it was a number that was already in her phone: Daniel's.

*You're hosting my sister, her boyfriend, AND me this weekend? Are you crazy?*

Emily responded quickly: *Only if you guys eat a lot. I work all week and won't have time to grocery shop.*

*Leave meal planning to me.*

Emily smiled. *I'll hold you to that.*

Kim Garrett entered the office, and Emily looked up.

"What were you smiling at your phone for?" her boss asked. Like Emily, Kim was tall and slim. Although Kim had three decades on Emily, the stately woman looked much younger than she was, and Emily envied the older woman's smooth, milk-chocolate-colored skin. With her thick, still-dark hair pulled neatly into a short, tightly curly ponytail, Kim could have spent her life posing for CoverGirl photo shoots instead of managing an inn.

"A couple of friends are coming up this weekend." Emily was still smiling and looking back down at her phone to make sure she hadn't missed anything. "I'll have three guests at my house."

"Will you have room?"

"Definitely," Emily replied. "It will be like a college dorm again. One of them is my friend Daniel—you know, the one who was here at the end of the summer for a few days?"

When Kim nodded, Emily stopped talking, leaned her elbow on the desk, and drummed her fingers against her chin in thought.

"Your wheels are turning," Kim said. "I can always tell when you're planning something because your nose crinkles up."

Emily laughed and crossed her eyes in a vain attempt to look at her nose. "It does not!" she protested.

"And you do that thing with your fingers." Kim nodded toward Emily's chin.

Emily looked at her hand and then dropped it to her lap. "That one, I know. I had the worst pimples on my chin in high school because that hand-to-face move is my go-to thinking posture!"

Kim leaned down to peck Emily on the cheek. The younger woman greatly appreciated that the inn owner relished her role as Emily's mom away from home.

"If you must know," Emily admitted, "I was just thinking that I'd invite my neighbor Suzie over when my friends are here this weekend. Daniel's single and she's single, they both do business things for a living, ..." She trailed off and again put her fingers to her chin.

"Stop meddling, little matchmaker," Kim playfully scolded.

"I guess I'm feeling romantic because I'm in 'wedding brain.'" Emily pointed to the paperwork on the desk.

"But," Kim continued, "isn't Daniel your childhood crush? Why would you want to fix him up with Suzie?"

Emily laughed. "Yeah, he was my crush when I was, like 8! He was always the 'older man.'" She paused and looked thoughtful. "Of course, he's grown into a very handsome older man, I must admit!"

"When you're in your 20s and there's less than 10 years' difference, that's not 'older man' status. Remember that I'm five years older than Milt." Kim paused. "Wait a minute: Suzie is the same age as you are!"

Emily could feel a light flush starting in her neck and moving upward. It was times like this that she hated having some of that Scandinavian heritage: every embarrassment showed on her face. Kim must have noticed because she thankfully changed the subject. Leaning over Emily's shoulder to look at the wedding checklist, Kim noted, "Everything is already checked off. You're pretty much done, aren't you?"

"This is a really nice couple," Emily said. "I want it to be done just right."

"Pshaw."

"Did you just say 'Pshaw'?" Emily laughed again.

"Yes, pshaw," Kim repeated. "Come on, you're done here. Let's go to the ballroom and finish checking out the decorations. Then it's lunch time for you!"

Emily and Kim walked down the hall together to the ballroom. Kim reached with both hands for the facing knobs of the double doors. The doors were white wood bordered with inset glass and covered by sheer curtains, but one couldn't really see what lie behind them.

When Kim opened the doors, both women gasped. The decorations team had outdone themselves. Emily knew that it was a fall outdoorsy theme because the couple had met in a hiking club two years earlier in November. But she had no idea how well that could be handled. The streamers and tablecloths were a light tan, and the table centerpieces featured flowers in strong oranges, browns, and yellows. The whole feeling was classy, yet comfortable. The large picture windows facing the mountains had only a short brown valence covering their tops, and Winter Wonderland Mountain looked like a wall-sized painting of Cezanne's famous Mont Sainte-Victoire peak in autumn. Orange sunlight splashed on the polished wood-paneled flooring.

"These guys are amazingly creative," Kim raved before Emily could say anything.

"I'm texting Suzie to come see this before the wedding starts this weekend." Emily began tapping on her cell phone. "Her sister is getting married next fall, and she has to check this out."

Kim chuckled. "Do that, and then go enjoy your lunch. And thanks for offering to do the afternoon at the front desk. It will really help having you show our two new employees how to handle a big group of people coming in for an event like this."

# CHAPTER SEVEN

"You are such a meddler." Emily's good friend Suzie gently batted Big Boy, the huge grey cat, off his perch on the arm of Emily's couch, plopped down, and curled her legs beneath her. She sipped her hot chocolate, used her forefinger to wipe the whipped cream off her upper lip, and then ineffectively tried to push her wild red hair out of her face. Emily noted, as she almost always did, that she wished her hair had even a tenth of the volume of her friend's.

"That's what Kim Garrett said!" Emily exclaimed. "That I'm a meddler."

"It's true," Suzie declared. "I can find my own dates, you know."

"I know. It's just that Daniel would be perfect for you."

"Why?" Suzie asked warily.

Emily tilted her head in thought. "I don't know. It's just that I like you both, so you must have a lot in common."

"Lame!" Suzie huffed. She dipped her spoon into her mug and pulled out mostly whipped cream. "I think there's more whipped cream in here than hot chocolate." She continued to dig around in her mug.

"What's more important?" Emily asked. "Anyway, stop changing the subject."

"I'll definitely help entertain your guests," Suzie promised. "But leave the fixing up alone. If it works out, then great."

"OK, but he's hot." Emily called up Daniel's Facebook photo and turned her phone for Suzie to see.

"He is." Suzie nodded. "But why don't you want him? What's wrong with him?"

Emily blew out a giggle that sent a puff of her own mug's whipped cream across the sofa and onto her friend's lap. "Sorry," she apologized as she jumped up to grab paper towels from the kitchen. She came back to the living room, trying to hold back a laugh at her cream-covered friend. "Daniel and I have been friends for years, so that would be weird." Emily handed the towels to Suzie.

As Suzie wiped her jeans, she shook her head. "Nope. That argument doesn't fly. You agreed with me a long time ago that it's better to be friends first."

"This is different, but I won't push." Emily took a breath and changed gears. "OK, the scoop is that we're taking them all to the Water Gap during the day on Saturday. What should we do Saturday night?"

There was a pause as the women sipped their drinks and thought. Then both their heads popped up at the same time and they yelled in unison, "*Apples to Apples!*"

"Perfect," Emily said. "That's, seriously, the best game to get to know what people are like. I haven't seen these guys in years, and Lauren's boyfriend is recent, as far as I can tell. This will be fun!"

"You do realize," Suzie said solemnly, "this makes us super-geeks."

Emily shrugged. "Hey, I can wear the geek name proudly!"

Saturday was cooler than anticipated, and Emily hoped her guests had planned their attire accordingly. She and Suzie had been taking turns looking out of Emily's kitchen window, which had a view of the parking lot of the apartment complex, for the past hour, since 10 a.m. Daniel had texted that they hoped to get off by 8. It was a two-hour ride, which meant they were now an hour late.

"I hope the tunnel wasn't too crowded." Emily gazed out the window and began chewing her lower lip. "Drivers slow down in there even though it stays two lanes."

"They're fine," Suzie assured, joining her at the window. "You said that Lauren's 21. Remember what we were like then. Lots of junk to pack!"

An emerald-green van pulled into the parking lot and quickly stopped. Daniel stomped out of the driver's seat. Even from the window, Emily could see that he was scowling.

Emily and Suzie ran down one flight of stairs to the parking lot to help their guests with their luggage. By the time the two women exited the back door to the apartment building, Daniel, Lauren, and a young man that Emily assumed was Jason already had their arms full. Daniel's scowl had morphed into a look of resignation, and although they all seemed a bit travel-weary, they each had looks of varying degrees of anticipatory excitement on their faces.

"Don't ask," Daniel said, as he gave Emily a quick one-armed hug, since his other arm bore three duffle bags. "Lauren changed her outfit three times."

"I don't know what good hiking clothes are," Lauren explained.

"I told her that it's just the shoes that matter." The young man with them put out his free hand. "Hi, I'm Jason."

"I'm Emily, and this is my friend Suzie." Everyone finished exchanging hellos, and then Emily led them up the back stairs to her apartment to assign their various sleeping areas.

"Sorry that you're on the couch, Daniel," Emily apologized.

"Oh, no," Daniel said, walking straight toward Emily's spare room. "I'm here as a favor, so I get the bedroom. Jason sleeps on the couch."

As Jason dropped his bag on Emily's couch, Daniel pulled Emily aside. "I'm not being a priss," he explained. "I'm testing to see how much he really likes my sister." His dark blue eyes flashed mischievously.

Emily grinned. "Sure you are!"

After they got settled and filled up several water bottles—and after Emily made them each put on a sweatshirt—they piled into the green van; it was the only vehicle that would comfortably hold five people. Daniel drove, and Emily asked Suzie to sit up front with him because she claimed she thought it would be awkward for her friend to sit in the back with the "youngsters." Suzie scrunched up her eyes and nose and gave Emily a "stop meddling" look, but Emily just smiled and lifted one shoulder.

The mountains were strutting their fall colors like runway models today, and Emily's guests were delighted. Bright oranges, reds, and yellows, along with light and dark shades of green and brown of the evergreens, bedecked the mountains on either side of the Delaware Water Gap. In fact, the drive to the hiking spot had them stopping for more photo ops than the hike itself. The trip down Route 115 always had the best views of the gap, which opened slowly like a lovely mottled theater curtain as they drew closer to it. The two small, mounded mountains pretended to be one at first, and then they gradually pulled apart like that curtain, with the blue and white sky brightening the changing landscape as the gap widened.

There was no shortage of topics to talk about, as old friends caught up and new ones got to know each other. Emily had planned a hike that would last no more than 2 hours, but although it was just late afternoon when they returned to the apartment, Jason went to Daniel's room and Lauren to Emily's to "crash." Even Suzie excused herself to go to her own apartment to take a "snappy nappy." She promised to be back in 90 minutes to join them for dinner.

Daniel threw himself on Emily's big black faux-leather recliner and immediately pulled the handle to lean back.

"Et tu, Brute?" Emily asked.

"A snappy nappy sounds like a good idea," Daniel protested. "I'm making dinner, and the chef gets to regenerate first."

"You're *making* dinner?" Emily asked. "I thought we'd just get pizza."

"I said I'd do meal planning." Daniel raised his chin. "Don't get too excited, though; it's just spaghetti and my dad's homemade meatballs, but I'm the one who took the initiative to ask him to make them for us!"

"Hey, I'm always excited about dinner no matter what it is or who made it," Emily confirmed, "as long as it's not me doing the work!"

# CHAPTER EIGHT

E mily had earlier explained that she was not a napper, but with her home filled with sleeping people, she figured she could sit on her comfy green couch and read the latest romance novel that she had downloaded from the library to her Kindle. Daniel ratcheted the recliner further back, and Emily fluffed a pillow in the corner of the sofa and settled in.

"Emily." A gentle tap on her shoulder made her realize that despite her arguments to the contrary, she really could be a napper. Daniel was crouched beside her, and she was sprawled sideways on her couch.

"Man, you were out." He smiled widely into her face as her eyes fluttered open. "I was clanging around making all sorts of noise looking for pots and pans, and you didn't stir."

Emily narrowed her eyes at him, but she didn't move. She was noticing just how deep blue Daniel's eyes were. Hers were blue, too, but they were the standard blonde-and-light-blue-eyed blue. His were like the blue of the sky late at night when the moon was full—dark blue but not black. And his eyes were twinkling.

Daniel blinked, probably because she was staring at him, she realized. She could feel her face grow pink, the curse of her pale Northern-European skin.

"Well, Miss 'I Hike Here All the Time,'" Daniel began, staying crouched by her head, "I guess we city folk wore you out."

Emily placed her palm on his chest and pushed him away, not without first noticing how solid his chest was. My, Daniel had truly grown into a strong man. He fell back on his heels as Emily sat up. "You did not wear me out," she protested. "I just had a long work week."

Daniel's face was below hers now, and he looked up at her, with a smile that Emily was sure was actually lighting up the darkening room. Then he popped up to a standing position, grabbed her hands from her lap, and pulled her to her feet. She bumped against him, and she realized he smelled good, like fall leaves.

"How come you don't stink?" she asked, still standing close to him.

"What?"

Emily put her nose against his chest and took an exaggerated sniff. "You smell like the woods, not like sweat."

She felt his chest rumble with what seemed like both a chuckle and a little shiver.

"We city boys don't sweat." He took a small step back. "We perspire."

"Ugh." Emily swatted his shoulder and pushed past him to the kitchen. "You didn't break anything, did you? Look, the water is boiling." She opened the box of spaghetti beside the pot and dumped it in.

"Oh, no you don't." Daniel hurried to her side. "You're going to take credit for cooking now, aren't you?"

"Of course." She laughed.

Daniel quickly stirred the pasta that she had tossed in. "You can be the sous-chef," he pretended to grumble.

Emily stepped away from the stove and tilted her head in a listening posture, trying to hear if there was any other movement in the apartment. "Hey, are Lauren and Jason still asleep?"

Daniel explained that his sister and her boyfriend had taken the van out to get dessert. "They saw that farmer's market at the end of your road, and it advertised pies."

Emily snorted a laugh and shook her head. She opened her refrigerator and pointed to two pies on the second shelf. "Well, we'll certainly have more than enough dessert!"

Suzie arrived just as Jason and Lauren were returning. Dinner was fantastic, and the taste of Daniel and Lauren's father's giant moist meatballs brought back memories of summer dinners at the shore—which Daniel, Lauren, and Emily proceeded to ramble on about to the others who "just had to have been there," as Lauren insisted. They quieted down, though, when dessert was served. The group had ended up with two apple pies, but Emily's second pie was pumpkin and Jason and Lauren had added a cherry, so there was plenty of variety. There were also a lot of "mm-mm good"-ing and other yummy-type sounds.

After stuffing their faces, they went to the living room, and Emily set out *Apples to Apples*. The game involved one player picking a card with an adjective on it and the other players discarding cards from their hands that contained noun phrases that best matched the adjective. The player who held the adjective card chose a noun card, from the other players' discarded cards, that he or she thought best fit the adjective card. The player whose card was chosen won the adjective card—and the round.

It was 11:30 p.m. by the time Daniel had picked "airline food" as the winning phrase to match his adjective "delicious."

"Seriously?" Lauren asked. "'Strawberry shortcake' was *my* card! How could you pick 'airline food' over 'strawberry shortcake'?"

Daniel shrugged as he handed his card to Jason, the winner with "airline food." "I recently took an Air France flight," he explained, "and the food was amazing!"

Lauren threw a sofa pillow at her brother's head.

"On that note, let's call it a night," Emily announced. "Church is at 9 a.m. tomorrow."

"Sounds good," Lauren said, gathering up the cards.

Daniel cleared his throat. "I'll bow out tomorrow, if that's OK."

Lauren gasped. "Danny, she's our hostess!"

"It's just not my thing." He took a moment to glare at his sister and then rearranged his expression to look hopefully at Emily. "I'll make a big breakfast for you all to eat when you come back."

"Um, I like to stay for Sunday school," Emily said, almost apologetically. "I guess you could make lunch instead."

"Danny!" Lauren chastised again.

Emily placed her hand gently on Lauren's arm. "That's fine," she said, still looking at Daniel. "Having a nice lunch when we come back is super." She leaned over to whisper to Lauren. "My dad always says, 'You can't force a person into the kingdom.'" Lauren nodded and sighed.

Because there was a lingering awkwardness, they all worked quickly to put the game away. Emily set up a sleeping bag and bed pillow on the couch, while Jason gave Lauren a quick kiss goodnight under the watchful eye of her brother. Then Daniel closed the door to the spare bedroom, and Lauren and Emily went to Emily's room.

"Sorry about Daniel and church," Lauren said, as the two women dressed for bed. "He's still mad at God for letting Matthew join the cult. It's painful for all of us, but Danny seems to take it the hardest. Those two were pretty close."

"Thanks for letting me know," Emily responded. "Sometimes, people have to work through their issues alone with God, and we can't get in the way."

"Matthew hardly talks to any of us anymore." Lauren sighed. "Every spare moment is spent with the cult recruiting or learning. If he does talk to us, it's usually to ask for money. Plus, because he takes his kids with him to a lot of the cult activities, we don't get to see our nieces very often. I think that's a big part of what is killing Daniel. He was really hoping to be the fun uncle."

"I'm so sorry." Emily climbed into her side of the bed and tucked the red flannel sheets up to her chin.

"Thanks." Lauren took her side of the bed. "And thanks for reminding me about what your dad said. I pray that Daniel will come around, but I often think that if I argue hard enough and loud enough, God will get it. And I know that's never right."

"It's probably more fun, though, right?" Emily said, allowing her guest off the hook. She heard Lauren giggle. Emily finished up with "Goodnight."

"Goodnight," Lauren echoed.

Emily turned off the bedside lamp and then prayed silently: *Dear God, please help me to be a good witness without pushing. Help me show Lauren and Daniel what a comfort you can be as they struggle with their brother's situation. And please, please, help Matthew find you.*

In the spare room, Daniel was having trouble sleeping. He hoped he hadn't been too obstinate about not wanting to go to church, but lately, he had begun to feel more and more uncomfortable in churches, even the few times he'd attended with his family on weekends when he visited them. He actually thought that he might have gone to the service with Emily the next day if she had pushed it, but it was better this way. And Emily seemed to be OK with it.

Emily was great. He was aware that she and Brandon had broken up, but he didn't know the circumstances and now he had to wonder what had happened. She would make some guy a great girlfriend. She was friendly and outdoorsy and cute. Actually, she was beautiful. She had those great eyes—the kind poets write about as limpid pools—and those long legs. And she was always smiling. That's what really made her remarkably pretty.

Daniel flopped to his other side. This was turning out to be a way better weekend than he expected.

# CHAPTER NINE

The next morning, Suzie joined the churchgoers, but she bowed out when it came time for the noon meal. "It smells amazing," she said, when she stopped with the rest of them at Emily's apartment before moving on to hers. Daniel had decided to go with more of a brunch, and when Emily opened her door, the scents of scrambled eggs and blueberry pancakes spilled into the hallway. Suzie sighed. "But I promised my folks I'd Skype them this afternoon."

They said their goodbyes to Suzie, and then Lauren asked, "Where did you find blueberries this time of year?"

"Frozen," Emily and Daniel replied in unison.

"I made sure I bought a refrigerator with a big freezer so that I could have frozen fruit after summer was over." Emily sat down at the already-set table and fanned out a napkin to place on her lap. "And summer isn't that long up here!"

The rest of them sat as well. Then they said a quick group prayer that they all knew from childhood, one that even Daniel joined in on, and dug into the meal.

Later, as Lauren waved away Jason's offer of yet another pancake, she turned to her brother. "Danny, why don't you make a big lunch for me like this every time I come home from college? I'd come home more often!"

"Because I don't *want* you coming home more often." Daniel stood and walked behind his sister's chair to tousle her hair. She swatted his hand.

"Listen, you guys are welcome back any time," Emily said. She leaned back in her chair, pushed her stomach out, and patted it. "Especially if you cook!"

"I can't cook at all," Jason confessed. "I can't even grill. I can make macaroni and cheese from a box; that's about it. And ramen noodles. Lauren bakes, though. Next time, have her make you her caramel brownies. I ate a whole batch by myself once!"

"Maybe my folks can have you over in the summer," Lauren suggested. "I know that Danny plans to ski with you in the winter, but because Jason and I will be in school, I won't be able to come. Plus, I kind-of hate the cold."

"You and me both!" Emily placed her hand over Lauren's. "I wear about 20 layers when I hit the slopes. And I take at least two lunch breaks!"

Daniel shook his head, and Emily caught his eye. "Don't worry," she assured him. "I promise to be a good ski buddy. I won't make you stay back with me when I'm skiing too slowly or whining about being freezing."

Daniel flashed her a smile. "I'm not worried at all. I remember that you were never timid about attacking the things the bigger kids did. You even came up with more-daring adventures than we could think up! You almost broke your leg the time you jumped off the back dock in Corolla! My mom always said you had 'spunk.' I'm sure you'll be tearing up the ski slopes right along with the rest of us!"

Emily crossed her arms and leaned her head back as if she were contemplating the thought. "I like 'spunk,' whether that's accurate or not." Then she bent forward and pointed at him. "As long as you don't call me 'brat' like you always did when we were little, I'm good."

Lauren groaned and then stood up. "Excuse me. I'm stuffed, but I have to go finish packing. You boys should too. We've got to get on the road no later than 2. Jason and I have to get back to school."

"I'm all set already," Daniel said, as Jason and Lauren went to get their things together. Emily had begun clearing the table, so he grabbed a few plates and followed her to the sink. "Hey, are you still planning to go see Jackson dance next month?"

They both lowered their dishes into the sink at the same time, and she turned to face him, her blue eyes wide with excitement. Daniel had the sudden thought that the look was so adorable that he had to kiss her. He shook his head and stepped back. Where did that come from?

Emily didn't seem to notice. "I would love if you'd come with me!" she nearly squealed. "It's the Saturday before Thanksgiving. Everyone else bailed on me. Two friends from church now have family things that weekend, Suzie can't go, and Brandon moved away. I do *not* want to drive to New York City by myself. If you go, I can drive to your place in Philly and then we can take the train. I'll stay with my folks over the weekend."

Daniel nodded and chuckled at her enthusiasm. "Let me check my calendar; that's not for a while, but I'm usually free around the holidays. Let me get back to you."

"Jackson can't get us a discount, but he can usually get decent seats together for a small group of people." Emily bounced on her toes, her excitement clearly continuing to grow. "Let me know if you have any friends who want to go, and I'll order the tics the week or two before." She clapped her hands together. "Oh, I hope it works out. I think it will be amazing!"

Daniel watched as Emily nearly skipped back to the table to get more dishes, and he thought that she just might be right.

E arly the next evening, after working the day shift, Emily popped down the hall to Suzie's apartment. Her friend had texted earlier in the day to say that she was in the mood for pizza dinner—from Benny's, of course—and needed to share it with someone.

"Extra cheese and mushrooms," Suzie said, as Emily followed her to the kitchen.

"I could smell it in my apartment." Emily smacked her lips. "My mouth has been watering since this morning when you mentioned this."

"Let's take it in the living room and watch *Modern Family* reruns." Suzie handed Emily a canned soda and a paper plate with two slices spilling over it.

Settled into Suzie's sofa, the two each said grace silently and then dug into a slice of pizza. With her mouth still full, and having not yet clicked on the TV, Suzie asked, "Well, you really thought you'd try to fix me up with Daniel?"

Emily's expression drooped. "You didn't like him?" She took a sip of soda to try to mask her disappointment.

Suzie smiled. "No, he's great. He's fantastic. He's polite. He's a great big brother. He's gorgeous." She paused, finished chewing, put down her plate, and stared at Emily. "And he's totally into you."

Emily nearly spewed her birch beer. "What?"

Suzie laughed. "I suspected that you didn't see it. And I think that's because you're into him too."

Emily tilted her head at her friend. "And you call me a romantic? You are seeing things where there are not, uh, things."

Both women laughed. "OK." Suzie pretended to admit defeat. "But think about it. You two seemed to get along well."

Emily turned her plate around and took a bite of her pizza crust. As she chewed, she considered Suzie's observations. "I did have a crush on Daniel my whole childhood," Emily conceded. "But only for one week every summer. Then it was back to real life, and I'd almost forget about him for months. A year later, we'd return to the Outer Banks, and he was once again the dreamiest guy in the world!"

Suzie shook her head. "Just saying." She reached for the remote and turned on her flat-screen TV.

Emily laughed, but she did have trouble concentrating on the plot of the sitcom episode she had seen a dozen times as Suzie's words tickled her musings. Could she even think about Daniel like that again? Suzie was right, of course: he *was* gorgeous, with that silky caramel-colored hair and those deep blue eyes that still had little gold specks that she used to love to stare at when she was younger—and when he was sitting still long enough to let her. But before this summer, she hadn't seen him in years. Now they were online "friends" and were enjoying messaging each other now and then about their days. She looked forward to those one-sentence catchups, but that was it.

Nah, that meant they were just friends, and that was nice.

Emily's phone tinged, and she saw that it was a Facebook message from Daniel. She glanced up at Suzie, looking surprised and grinning. "It's from Daniel. It's almost as if he knew we were talking about him." Suzie shook her head again, and Emily noted that her friend was doing that a lot lately.

*Thanks for a great weekend. Looking forward to NYC. I'm trying to get two friends to join us. I'll let you know.*

Emily let out a relieved breath. "See." She held up her phone. "He's bringing other friends to the ballet. There's nothing there."

# CHAPTER TEN

Texts

Daniel: *Thanks again for a great weekend, Emily. Did you see Lauren's photos of our trip? When did she take all those pictures?*

Emily: *I don't know. :-) I like her nature shots, but we look like lazy lumps in the photo she took in my living room. And was the room really that messy?*

Daniel: *YOU do not look lazy in that pic, but the rest of us do! You crack me up. You smile even when you're exhausted.*

Emily: *That is a grimace! My legs were killing me!*

Emily straightened the horn of plenty one more time on the big, round, glass table in the lobby of Sweet Fern Inn. The Garretts knew that not all their guests were fans of Halloween, so Kim Garrett had decided to use lots of fall-themed decorations this year instead of emphasizing ghosts and skeletons. She relied on Emily to handle most of the design, and Emily had taken several ideas from the fall-themed wedding a few weeks earlier. The vases of summer flowers—and, of course, the long sweet ferns—had made way for dried cattails, grasses, and thistles. Linens on the side tables were made up of browns and reds and yellows to reflect the colors of the changing leaves outside that guests could see from the front doors, the restaurant's big picture windows, and the windows in the individual rooms. Cinnamon-scented pinecones in bowls around the lobby added a sweet-and-spicy aroma. The air had cooled, and guests and employees alike traversed the inn wearing sweaters.

The phone on the front desk rang, and Emily listened surreptitiously to the new girl, Stacey, speak to the customer on the other end of the line.

"Yes, we have a king room available that weekend in February," Stacey said. "We have discount tickets to the slopes if you're coming for a ski trip. Wonderful. Yes, you can do that all online."

Emily smiled and headed to the front desk. Stacey was a winner. The young college woman looked up, which made her dark brown ponytail start swinging slightly. "I think that will be the last room booked for that same weekend in February when your friends are coming," she told Emily. "You guys are going to have so much fun."

"I know, and I can't wait." Emily beamed. As she walked away, though, she bit her lower lip. She had thought a lot about that weekend over the past few weeks, and although she was excited, she had begun to get a little nervous. She loved to ski and knew she'd have fun with Danny, but he was bringing several of his work friends —all guys. Would she feel out of place? Would they expect her to be or act a certain way? Would they think she was Danny's girlfriend? She and Danny had been messaging and texting more often these days; maybe she should tell him about her concerns.

She shrugged and shook her head. She'd be seeing him in a couple of weeks when they went to see the ballet, so she could approach the subject then. She didn't want it to seem like a big deal. Danny was her friend, and he'd make sure she was comfortable.

∾

**T**exts

Daniel: *I'm bringing my friends Paul and Marissa to the ballet. Check them out on my Facebook. I want to pay for everyone's tickets, including yours. Let me arrange it through Jackson.*

Emily: *No way. I can pay for my own ticket!*

Daniel: *I know, but I already called Jackson last night, and it's a done deal. Row M, center, 4 tics. Plus, he's giving us a backstage tour afterward. See you next week.*

Emily: *Then I'm buying the intermission hot chocolate!*

Daniel: *Deal!*

~

**D**aniel was looking forward to the following week's trip to New York. They had decided on a matinee so that they could maximize their time in the city. They would all be leaving by car from Marissa's place, which was only about 10 blocks from Daniel's. Emily planned to arrive at 9:30 in the morning. That way, she could park in Daniel's spot in the underground garage in his condo complex and the two of them could walk to Marissa's apartment together. He would take out his car the night before to find a parking place on the street.

Lifting his feet now to set them on his coffee table, Daniel leaned back on the sofa and balanced his dinner plate on his stomach. It was times like this that he loved living alone. It was late, well past 9 p.m., and he'd had a long day, so it was nice not to have to talk to anyone. He called up on his DVR the past weekend's Philadelphia Eagles' game. Because he'd already seen it, he wouldn't have to pay too much attention while he ate the slices of pork loin that he had grilled up.

He liked his condo, he thought absently, chewing and looking around. It was "manly without being impersonal," his mother had claimed when she and his sister helped him pick out furnishings and direct where things should go on his walls. He had a lot of family photos, and his glance stopped on a framed shot of Matthew's oldest daughter holding her new little sister. He sighed and shook his head. *They're probably in a weirdo church service right now, worshiping that creepy old lady,* he thought. *Those poor little kids. Mom thinks that things will change when Mercedes goes to nursery school next year. Either way, both those girls are going to need a lot of therapy when they grow up!*

Thinking of the girls made him think of Emily. She had told him that she was praying for Matthew's family. Although he doubted it would help, it seemed like a kind thing to do that Emily would follow through on.

Emily's smiling face popped into his head, and he grinned himself as he remembered that he'd be seeing her smile in a few days. As he thought about her, though, his smile faded a bit. He had begun wondering a lot lately about what Paul and Marissa would think of his relationship with Emily. It would have been better if one of the other guys or even one of Emily's friends had decided to join them for the ballet. With just the two of his friends coming along— and those two were clearly a couple—it now seemed too much like a double date with him and Emily. Daniel was concerned that Marissa might say something to embarrass Emily. Maybe he should ask Paul to explain everything to Marissa before the two women met each other.

His phone rang, which surprised him because very few of his friends ever called these days; they all texted. His cell was vibrating in a small circle on the table in front of him, and he saw that it was Emily. He put his near-finished dinner plate on the coffee table and picked up the phone—because, sure, living alone was great, but talking to Emily would be just as great.

"Hey, Em."

"I am really psyched about next week." Emily was nearly effervescing. "I just got off the phone with Jackson. After he gives us his 'private backstage tour,' he said he'd join us for dinner. He knows a good but inexpensive-for-New-York restaurant near the Lincoln Center."

Daniel imagined what Emily looked like as she talked to him, her blue eyes sparkling with passion and her long, slim fingers drawing pictures in the air as she spoke. He smiled more broadly.

"Are you sure that won't put you out too late?"

"No, I'm staying overnight at my folks, and I have a key to their house," Emily explained. "I promised them that I'd tiptoe on the way in. Their church service isn't until 11 the next day, I'll get enough sleep."

"You don't have to work on Sunday?"

"Nope. I'm working Thanksgiving, and the Garretts were fine with letting me take off this whole coming weekend."

Daniel groaned. "You have to work on Thanksgiving? Bummer."

"Aw. That's sweet that you feel sorry for me!" Emily laughed. "It's the nature of the hospitality business. I only have to work that Thursday, though. I have the next day off. My parents and Abby and Aaron are coming here for a belated Thanksgiving celebration on Friday. It actually works out great because Aaron has a girlfriend and he can go to her family's house on Thursday. Then I don't have to work again until Sunday."

"OK, then." Daniel drew out those two words. He didn't want to hang up quite yet.

"How about you?" Emily seemed to want to keep the conversation going as well. "What are you doing for Thanksgiving?"

"Oh, my folks always do a big thing. Everybody lands at our house: grandparents, the three aunts, my one cousin Karen who's still in college nearby. We stuff our faces and then watch football. It's very American!"

"Does your brother Matthew come?"

"Of course not!" Daniel spat out, not holding back his anger. "Their cult says that Thanksgiving worships the wrong god. I have no idea where that idea comes from, but I think it's one more way to keep their members away from family. In fact, I think the group members all get together and celebrate their own weird brand of giving thanks."

"I'm sorry, Daniel."

"Yeah, well, we've gotten used to it, I guess," Daniel said. "Sorry I snapped."

"I get it." There was another pause, and Emily let out a reluctant sigh. "Well, I've got to get to sleep to save energy for this weekend."

"Me, too," Daniel agreed, brightening. "It's gonna be a blast."

# CHAPTER ELEVEN

Two days later, Emily woke up early to go to the gym. Before she headed to the car, she began setting up her phone to listen to her latest audio book. It was then that she noticed that Daniel had texted her the night before. She had been exhausted and hadn't even thought to look at texts before diving into bed.

*Quick question,* the text read.

Emily texted back now: *Sorry, I crashed last night.*

She got an immediate response from Daniel: *What's the dress code for the ballet? Marissa made Paul ask me to ask you. What are we? 12 years old?*

*What are you doing awake?* Emily texted. *It's 6 a.m.*

*Early meeting to prepare for. Are you in the mood for a quick call?*

*Sure.*

Emily's cell rang, and she answered, "Theater casual."

"What?"

"That's the dress code," Emily said, laughing. "It's a matinee, so it's not super-formal, but I'm wearing a nice blouse and dress pants, like I'd wear to a business meeting."

"Do I have to wear a tie?"

"Tie optional."

"Whew." Daniel released a dramatic whistle of relief. "No tie, then. Thanks."

Emily snickered and then grew serious. "Uh, Daniel?'

"Yeah?"

"I've been meaning to ask you something." She hesitated. "Do you have a few minutes to talk before your meeting?"

"Plenty of time," he replied. "Is everything OK?"

"Oh, yes." Emily took a silent deep breath to fortify herself and said a little prayer. Then she continued, "Would you mind telling me a bit about what's up with your brother? You don't have to if you don't want to," she finished hurriedly.

Daniel sighed. "I don't mind talking about it. People ask about it all the time, especially because Matthew has kids, which means I have nieces. Everyone wants to know more about the girls." He paused. "And when I say 'everyone,' I mean women. Women seem fascinated with the fact that there are little kids in my life."

Emily let out a quick snort.

"I don't mean to come across as sexist," Daniel defended himself, "but they always want to see pictures and ask if I love doting on them, and I just always say sure because I don't feel like having to explain why it's not that easy to do."

"I get it," Emily empathized.

"It's not the girls' fault. I know that. But it's hard to embrace the whole uncle thing when their parents have been so incredibly hurtful to my family."

Emily made a humming sound in agreement. "And by pushing the idea that the only thing that matters is how adorable the kids are," she said, "it dismisses the pain that you feel. It's as if they're saying you have no right to be hurt and angry."

"Wow. You *do* get it. I know it's selfish ..." He trailed off.

"It's how you feel," Emily stated plainly. "When Paige died, some people tried to tell me that I should be happy because she was in heaven with Jesus. When they said that, it implied I was being selfish for grieving for her."

Emily stopped for a moment as she remembered the pain of the sadness and the guilt that she used to feel and that her supportive pastor had helped her work through.

Daniel stayed quiet, just letting her remember.

"What I learned in the end was that I could both grieve and rejoice, and that God was with me through it all," Emily said, and then she took a deep breath and changed her tone. "Bottom line: tell those women to go fly a kite. It's none of their business anyway!"

Daniel and Emily laughed together, and then Emily went on. "The reason I want to know is, well, it's for my prayer life. I pray for Matthew regularly, but sometimes it's easier to pray when I know more details."

"OK, then, you asked for it," Daniel began. "Matt was kind of floundering. He had been working at a job for five or six years, but his friends were moving away or getting into relationships, and he felt left out. He had known Mary Rose from college, but at this point, she was in the Marines."

"The Marines?"

"Yeah," Daniel affirmed. "The cult creeps recruited her right on the base where she was serving!"

"Oh, my," Emily said quietly.

"It all happened pretty quickly. Matt went down to visit her one weekend, and she had her friends 'love bomb' him. That's what it's called when cult members try to recruit you. Trust me, in the beginning, I read a ton of books about what they call 'controlling groups.' Anyway, Matt came back home and said that he had found his true family and friends in this 'church.'" Daniel said the last word with disgust. "It's not a church. It's a bunch of lost young adults worshipping a Korean woman as god. They claim her husband was the second coming of Christ, but she's now their 'god in the flesh.'"

Daniel scoffed, and Emily could tell he was starting to get frustrated as he told the story.

But he wasn't finished. "He's dead, by the way," Daniel spat out. "The second-coming-of-Christ guy. And now they claim he's the spirit of god because he died. Really, you can't make this stuff up!"

"Oh, Daniel, I'm really sorry." Emily was glad they weren't Skyping so that he couldn't see the tears that had begun to trickle down her cheeks. Her heart broke for Daniel and his family, especially his parents. How must they feel after living their whole lives one way and training up their children "in the right way" (Proverbs 22:6)—only to have one of them respond like this?

"It's just stupid," Daniel said, and Emily could tell he was trying to sum up his pain. "It stinks for my parents because of the cult's whole 'no holidays' and 'don't be influenced by unholy family' and all that. All the anti-cult books say you should just act as if everything is OK. They say people like Matt and Mary Rose will see that *you* offer unconditional love and the cult doesn't. My folks went to lots of support groups, and they've even stopped calling it a cult to Matt's face. That's what the books advise you to do. So my folks just act 'supportive.' And, of course, they pray all the time. Like *that* has any power."

"Oh, Daniel," Emily said again.

"Sorry, Emmy." Daniel's voice was firm and not very apologetic. "I know your faith is important to you. But it seems to me that God has sort of gone all hands-off on this situation. My whole family—and their church—have been praying for years, and I guess God has decided this isn't important enough for Him."

"Do you remember the old movie *Shadowlands*?" Emily asked. "Our youth group watched it once, and I bought the DVD."

There was a pause, and Emily could tell that Daniel was surprised by what seemed like a big shift in the conversation.

"Never heard of it."

"Anthony Hopkins plays C.S. Lewis, whose wife is dying of cancer," Emily explained patiently. "She goes into remission, and one of Lewis's colleagues—not a Christian, I think—makes a comment like 'I guess your prayers changed God's mind.'"

"OK." Daniel clearly was waiting for Emily's point.

"Lewis has a great line." Emily could hear her own voice raise as she grew more excited. "He says, 'Oh, I don't pray to change God. I pray to change me.' Daniel, sometimes, that's the only thing that keeps me sane when I don't understand things like why Matt is in a cult or why Paige died. I pray to change me."

Daniel didn't respond, and Emily wasn't sure if he had hung up. "Danny?" she asked.

"Yeah?"

"Sorry for getting so deep this early in the morning," Emily said. "I'm just telling you what works for me. And I was thinking it might help you to understand where your parents are coming from."

"No, I get it. Thanks. That makes sense. I'm just not there yet. Maybe someday. I just don't get the why."

Emily chuckled ruefully. "And neither did Job."

"Job?"

"A discussion for another day." Emily laughed again. "Thanks for all this. I'm armed to the teeth for tonight's devotions!"

"Hey, glad I could help, I guess," Daniel said. "See you next week."

"Like you said, it's gonna be great!"

# CHAPTER TWELVE

Because Emily was 15 minutes early for their trip to New York, Daniel invited her into his condo for a cup of coffee before they traipsed off to Marissa's apartment. It had gotten considerably colder in the past week, meaning that even the short walk would be extra brisk. She agreed they needed fortification.

"What time did you wake up this morning?" Daniel asked after she had taken off her coat and he was leading her to his kitchen. He pointed her to a high-top chair at the grey-granite island. Emily studied him as he moved around the kitchen to get their coffees ready. He looked handsome in his tan sport coat, dark brown pants, and dark green shirt. No tie, she noticed.

"I was up around 6:30." Emily settled herself on the chair. "My schedule is always weird anyway, and I just go to bed when I need to in order to get seven or eight hours of sleep before I have to get up. Of course, I still use the alarm on my phone."

"Do you go right to sleep?" Daniel handed her a travel mug of coffee and sat on the other stool beside her.

Emily nodded.

Daniel groaned. "I'm jealous," he said. "I always have a hundred things swimming in my head. It can take me up to an hour to get to sleep."

Emily smiled and lowered her head.

"What?"

"When we were little," she began, lifting her head, "my father used to tell my mom that the reason he went to sleep right away was that he had a 'clear conscience.'" She looked at Daniel and wiggled her eyebrows mischievously. "Anything you need to confess?"

Daniel laughed. "Just that I work too hard!"

Emily tilted her head to study him. His dark blue eyes were flashing with amusement, but they were also full of some intense emotion that she couldn't quite define. Lately, those eyes were reminding her of the ocean on a sunny day, reflecting the sky and holding wonderful secrets.

She felt her breath hitch, stunned at that little tangent her mind had taken her on. But she recovered quickly. "You know, I love my job too." She poked his arm. "But remember that work isn't everything. I know you're just joking around, but you have to take care of yourself. It's not all about work. That's why I love my church. I can get involved in totally unrelated things there and hang out with totally different friends."

Daniel seemed to concentrate intently on his next sip of coffee.

"Sorry," Emily said, although she knew it wasn't exactly a heartfelt apology. "I know church isn't your thing. My point is that you have to make sure you get out enough to just have fun. And going to the gym doesn't count!"

"It's not that church isn't 'my thing.'" Daniel shook his head. "I'm actually not sure why I want to explain why I feel like I do, but whatever. It's just that I am really mad at God for the way He has handled the whole situation with Matthew. My brother is in a cult, for heaven's sake. That certainly can't be God's will. And yet God allows it."

Emily sighed and reached across the counter to put her hand on Daniel's arm. "I understand." She spoke softly. "I do. And I agree that it's not God's will that Matthew is in that cult. In fact, it's Matthew's own free will at work; it's your brother's choice. And it's a wrong one. What I believe is that God is crying *with* you over Matthew. And I believe God is working day and night to change him. I continue to pray that Matthew's heart and mind will be opened."

Daniel nodded, but it was clear to Emily that although he wasn't convinced, he didn't want to continue the conversation. He stood up and reached a hand to her. She took it and stood as well.

"I just don't think God's working hard enough," Daniel said with a shrug. "Here. Take a lid for your mug. We should start walking now."

Emily smiled as he led her to the living room. She squeezed Daniel's hand. When she let go, she picked up her coat, which she had thrown on the back of a chair, and watched Daniel go to a closet and take his own coat from there and put it on. She heaved a silent sigh. *God, help me reach Daniel,* she prayed. *He knows you; he's just really hurting and doesn't understand. You are God, and we don't always know your ways. But please give Daniel some joy so that he understands where all good gifts come from and that he can reach out to you in hope for his brother.*

They walked outside together in comfortable silence, huddled close against the chilly morning air. When they reached Marissa's home, Daniel introduced Emily to his best friend's girlfriend. Marissa hugged Emily and then leaned back to assess her.

"I love your hair," Marissa gushed. "It's a wonderful cut for your face. You have great high cheekbones, and the trim toward your face frames it perfectly."

"Thank you." Emily could feel a little warmth fanning her cheeks. Being blonde, blue-eyed, and fair-skinned, she was a fast and obvious blusher.

"Marissa is a hairdresser," Daniel explained as he put a reassuring hand on the small of Emily's back. "She cuts my hair, and she's always telling me I should do more with it."

"His choice of cut is too severe." Marissa scowled. "Even for a banker."

Shaking his head, Daniel waved a hand toward her dismissively. "You know I'm not a banker."

Marissa beamed victoriously, as if she teased him all the time about this very thing. "And I'm a hair *stylist*," she argued, "not a hair-dresser!"

One arm still around Emily, Marissa led her to sit on the couch. Daniel took the armchair. "Anyway, Emily," Daniel said, clearly trying to change the subject away from his own locks, "wasn't your hair a lot blonder when we were kids? I remember it was really, really light."

"Nice going, gentleman," Marissa chastised.

Emily laughed. "You only saw me in the summer," she said. "I was on swim team. Between the sun and the chlorine, I'm lucky my hair didn't turn completely white and fall out!"

Marissa gasped and finger-combed the side of Emily's head. "Your poor hair!"

Then Marissa turned abruptly on the couch, grabbed Emily's hands, and began bombarding her with questions. Emily warmed quickly to the other woman. They talked about their families, jobs, and apartment living. Out of the corner of her eye, Emily occasionally caught Daniel just watching them in silence for the half-hour before Paul showed up.

"She's a keeper," Marissa declared to Paul as he put out his hand to shake Emily's. Marissa leaned over to peck her boyfriend on the cheek and added, in a faux whisper, "She's a Christian. She may even get Daniel here back to church!"

Emily chuckled a little uneasily. It was slightly disconcerting that Paul and Emily seemed to be assuming, as she had feared, that she was Daniel's girlfriend. However, she was glad to know that his two friends were as concerned for his relationship with God as she was.

Daniel crossed to the door, where the introductions were taking place. "Emily has been my *friend* for years," he said, emphasizing the "friend" part. "I'll definitely keep her." He gave Emily's upper arm a playful punch. "Although I did want to throw her in the ocean during those awkward middle-school years."

Emily crossed her arms in mock affront. "You loved it! In fact, I distinctly remember the one time you got a girl to give you her phone number on the beach because she thought you were being all sweet and nice to me, 'your cute little sister.'" Emily used a cocked head and high, flirty voice to imitate the teenager who had taken a liking to Daniel those many years ago, which had, of course, infuriated her at the time. Now she turned to the others. "He offered me a dollar to pretend for the rest of the week that I really was his little sister. I didn't mind it." She looked over at Daniel and batted her eyes teasingly. "It gave me more time with *Danny*."

Paul and Marissa laughed. "C'mon, *Danny*," Paul said, herding them all out the door. "We're going to New York with Little Sis."

# CHAPTER THIRTEEN

The two-hour ride to New York was a blast. Shortly after they got out of Philadelphia and on to I95, Marissa suggested the alphabet game to pass time. The travel game involved searching for words on signs that started with each letter of the alphabet, and they had to find the letters in alphabetical order. By the time they reached the New Jersey turnpike, they had gone through the alphabet once, having skipped Q because they weren't finding anything. Emily then decided that singing old camp songs would keep them moving. They exhausted their repertoire just about the time they reached the Lincoln Tunnel. The passengers agreed to stay quiet from then on to enable Paul, their driver, to concentrate.

They lucked out and had no trouble finding a parking lot near the Lincoln Center. They were an hour-and-a-half early, so they grabbed sandwiches from Dunkin' Donuts a block away and walked in and out of the stores in the area, partly to see the merchandise and partly to stay warm. Then they strolled back to the center in plenty of time to go into the theater.

They climbed the steps to the plaza area of Lincoln Center, where three performing arts buildings surrounded a large circular fountain that guarded the center in stately pride. Streams of water pulsed from the center of the fountain. Despite the cold, scores of theatergoers basked in the unusual sunny November air.

"Oh, my," Marissa gasped. "I feel as if I don't deserve to be here!"

Daniel crossed his arms. "This is a huge complex," he noted.

"This area is 16 square acres," Paul declared.

The others turned in unison to stare at him, and he held up his phone. "I just looked it up," he admitted.

Emily grabbed Marissa's hand and squeezed it. "Isn't it gorgeous?" she agreed. "Our building for the ballet is the one on the left—it's called the Koch Theater, I remember. Look up. See those gorgeous outdoor light fixtures on the second floor, the promenade? Wait until you see them from inside looking out. Every time I look at them, I always gasp and then realize that I'm underdressed!"

Daniel smiled at Emily. She caught his eye and smiled back, having to tilt her head only slightly to meet his gaze. "What are you smiling at?" she asked.

"You're in your element."

"You can take the girl out of the city," Emily said with a grin, "but you can't take the city out of the girl. I may be living in the Poconos, but that doesn't mean that I can't appreciate all that city life has to offer."

Daniel leaned over and kissed the top of her head. Emily lowered her face to hide her blush, but he could see the pink right to the top of her head. It made him happy that he could affect her that way.

After entering the building and doing the requisite gasp at the chandeliers, and adding another group gasp at the view behind them through the floor-to-ceiling windows that let in the light from the plaza, the four made their way to their seats. They were in the front row of the second section on the floor, so they had room to stretch their legs, which both tall men appreciated.

"I'm glad they have the synopsis in the program," Paul admitted after they had settled in. "We had to read *Romeo and Juliet* in high school, and I didn't remember anything except that they all died at the end. Marissa was nice enough not to tell you, but I was a little afraid that this might be too girly. But, hey, this says there's fighting and insults and all sorts of action."

"And humor," Emily added. "I had a great lit professor in college who pointed out all the funny lines. The review of this ballet in the *New York Times* said that the choreography really nailed all the elements of humor and tragedy. I can't wait."

As the lights dimmed, Daniel chimed in, in a whisper. "Jackson told me he's only in, like, two or three of all the performances they're putting on. Apparently, this show is exhausting!"

Jackson had the role of Romeo, which was an amazingly demanding role for a dancer. He was on stage most of the show, and he was mesmerizing, as was the rest of the company. The production was top-notch across the board, and at intermission, Emily raved about the costuming.

"Did you notice how they are handling the colors?" she asked the rest of the group. "The Montagues are in hues of blue, and the Capulets have on yellows and light greens."

"I will definitely pay attention to that when we go back in," Daniel promised. "What I've been focused on is just how athletic everyone is. I mean I always knew that about Jackson, but they are all like that. You can see every muscle in their bodies! And how do the girls stay on their toes like that?" He made an attempt at going en pointe and nearly knocked Paul over.

Bells chimed in the hallway, indicating that the second act was to begin. As the men had each finished off their hot chocolates earlier, the women each took one last swig, threw the cups away, and headed back to their seats.

When the performance was over, a very sweaty but beaming Jackson met them by the inside stage door and then took them all backstage to see the set and meet the other dancers. The four friends were in awe, and Jackson smiled bashfully. "Isn't it amazing what they do with the sets?" he asked.

"Talk about amazing!" Daniel replied. "How do you get such flex-ibility?"

"Hours and hours of Pilates," Jackson admitted frankly and without guile.

Paul leaned to Daniel and stage-whispered, "I think we have to consider taking those Pilates classes being offering in the spring at our gym! Then we might look like him!"

They all laughed. Then Jackson leaned over to kiss Emily on the cheek, clearly being careful not to sweat on her. "Emily is wonderfully supportive," he told the rest of the group. "Next to my parents, she acts like my biggest fan." He looked at Daniel pointedly. "She is a good friend."

Daniel nodded. "I know," he agreed. Emily smiled at him, and he got a warm feeling in his chest.

They waited outside while Jackson changed and then walked to the restaurant that he had suggested, a small, out-of-the-way pub that seemed to be frequented mostly by the actors, singers, and dancers that entertained New York City. The group ordered seven or eight appetizers—one of each on the menu—and munched and talked for hours, until Jackson finally said that he had to go home to rest up for a rehearsal the next day.

After they hugged the dancer goodbye, the rest of them walked quietly in the dark to the car to head back to Philadelphia. Climbing into the back seat and leaning back, Emily let out a long "Whoa!" The other three laughed in agreement.

"That was magical!" She sighed. "There's no other word."

Marissa was already sitting beside her in the rear of the car, and Daniel notice that Marissa had grabbed Emily's hand. He was glad the women were getting along this well. "I agree," Marissa said. "What talent! What a production!"

"I'm still stunned at how he gets his legs to do those things," Paul said. "How does he not fall over?"

The ride home was quiet, and by the time they got back to Marissa's apartment, the women had fallen asleep. Paul parked the car, and he and Daniel turned from the front seat to look at Emily and Marissa.

"Isn't Marissa beautiful?" Paul observed. "I am truly lucky."

"Yes, you are, my man," Daniel agreed, clapping his friend on the shoulder.

"I think you've got a winner there, too, in Emily."

Daniel looked at his friend. "We're not ..."

"I know, I know," Paul interrupted. "You're just friends. But you may want to rethink that position." He opened the car door, and the inside roof light blinked on.

The women stirred, and Emily opened her eyes. Their usual bright blue was muted in the dimness of the car, and they seemed filled with warmth and something else. Friendship? Compassion? Something more? She smiled broadly at Daniel. He felt his heart melt a little. Her wool dress coat was buttoned up to her chin, and her blonde hair was mussed and clinging in different angles to the back seat. She looked adorable. He wondered: Could Paul be right?

# CHAPTER FOURTEEN

I t had been several weeks since Stacey had started working at the front desk at Sweet Fern Inn, and Emily was thrilled at the way their new employee was settling in. Stacey was in her senior year of college, majoring in hotel, restaurant, and tourism management at East Stroudsburg University, only a half-hour's drive from the inn, and Emily was praying that the young woman would want to stay on as a full-time front-desk staff member after graduation in May.

Stacey's efficiency had freed up Emily to do more with the event planning team such as organizing fun holiday activities, from home-away-from-home entertainment at Thanksgiving, through Christmas-themed December weekends, to the inn's big New Year's Eve party.

Emily's first attempts at arranging activities on her own came to fruition over Thanksgiving weekend. Her goal for Thanksgiving Day at Sweet Fern was to make sure guests felt extra welcome since they were not going to be in their own homes for the holiday. In the morning, she led children's games such as bobbing for apples and drawing hand turkeys. She double-checked that the scents of cinnamon, apples, and pinecones were filling the halls and common rooms and keeping everyone in a holiday mood. Then, throughout the afternoon, the restaurant had timed seatings at which the hotel guests could eat a traditional Thanksgiving meal, and Emily made sure she visited each table to determine that all their holiday needs were being met. She had even asked the chef to offer "tofu turkey" for those who didn't eat meat.

For the Friday after Thanksgiving, even though it would be a day off for Emily, she had talked the chef into preparing a menu selection of standard Thanksgiving "leftovers," including turkey sandwiches on white bread with mayonnaise, which several of the staff members admitted were their favorites. She was especially proud of those plans, knowing that the guests would either need bagged meals for a long day of Black Friday shopping at the outlet stores or would be just lounging around wanting the ambience to feel comfortable and familiar. When Emily left the inn on Thursday evening, she was exhausted but pleased with the way the weekend events were working out.

At her own apartment Friday morning, she slept in just as she had told Daniel she would. Her family wasn't expected to arrive at her place until 2, and as she did every year, she had warned everyone that although she was hosting, she wouldn't actually be cooking. For the past three years, Emily had paid Chef Tony to make a complete Thanksgiving meal for Emily to take home on Thursday evening, which just required a heating up two hours before serving. She did her own decorating, and yes, she had prepared hors d'oeuvres herself and frozen them earlier in the week. But she liked to say that she always let the professional do the big stuff! Her parents would be bringing their traditional sausage stuffing, and her sister and brother, Abby and Aaron, were in charge of desserts.

Emily padded around her apartment in her flannel PJs and warm socks until a little after noon. At that point, she placed the turkey and the fixings into her oven—one of the selling points of this apartment complex was that each kitchen had a full-size oven—and changed into her favorite fleece-lined khakis from L.L. Bean and a turtleneck with an interlacing fall-leaf pattern of oranges and browns. Then she sat down to read.

Emily's sister Abby arrived with their parents shortly before 2. "Oh, my gosh," Abby gushed as she walked in with a pie and a tin of what Emily knew had to be homemade peanut brittle. "It smells heavenly in here!"

Emily hugged her big sister. Abby was the same height as Emily, but she was broader and stronger. Emily loved when the two of them hugged because she felt extra protected.

"It smells like heaven thanks solely to Tony," Emily admitted.

"But you're a good heater-upper," Emily's mother declared, embracing her daughter as soon as the sisters broke apart.

When Aaron finally arrived a half-hour later, Abby mussed her twin brother's hair and teased, "Nice of you to join us."

Emily chimed in. "We've been toiling over a hot stove, and you waltz in with a store-bought pie!"

"Hey, I mostly made this myself," Aaron protested. "I put the canned pumpkin stuff into a prepared pie crust, but I did, in fact, have to bake it in my own oven! And I did bring two cans of whipped cream. OK, that I bought."

Emily's eyes grew big. The pie did look really good.

"You actually know how to turn on an oven?" Abby asked, continuing to needle her brother.

The rest of the meal preparation time involved similar teasing, but when they sat down to eat, they quieted.

"May I say grace?" their mom asked.

"Of course," Emily replied.

"Dear God," Jan Steverman began, "we thank you for all the blessings of this past year. We thank you for health and family and friends. For good jobs. For your constant support. We miss Paige, but we thank you for the years you gave us with her, and we hope you and she are having a wonderful Thanksgiving as well! Thanks for this wonderful food, and help us be mindful of those who are hungry. Amen."

"Amen!" the rest of the family echoed.

They all tried to be polite and take the dining experience slowly, but that didn't last long, as they fairly quickly chucked all pretenses and chowed down on the turkey and all the fixings. It wasn't very long before they were stuffed, as usual, and they agreed to wait a bit for dessert. Each eater said back in their chair at the table to let the food settle.

"So how's Daniel?" Abby asked Emily after a few moments of comfortable silence.

"Daniel?" Emily sat forward, a bit surprised. "Fine, I guess."

"C'mon Emmy, I know you talk to him a lot," Abby pushed. "I'm friends with that whole gang on Facebook!"

Emily shrugged. "I guess I do. We do text a lot. He really has become a good friend over the past few months."

"A good friend?" Aaron asked, eyebrows raised. "What does that mean?

Emily blushed and threw her napkin at her brother. "What? Don't you have any friends, Aaron?"

"Not ones that I pined after every single summer!"

Emily could feel her face getting even redder, so she rose and picked up a few plates to take to the kitchen. "For heaven's sake," she scoffed. "Just because you fall in love every few months with a different girl doesn't mean that's what I'm doing."

Emily ignored Aaron's protests, keeping her back to him as she walked to the kitchen. When she placed her dishes in the sink, she felt her sister sidle up beside her and add dishes to Emily's pile.

"Seriously," Abby whispered. "Anything there?"

Emily turned toward her sister. She leaned back against the sink, sighed, and then chewed on her lower lip. "I'm not sure," she finally admitted to both Abby and herself. "I really enjoy his company. I love talking to him all the time, and I miss it when we can't connect. He's such a great guy."

There was a pause. "But ..." Abby coaxed.

"You know my faith is important to me. And Daniel has a lot of baggage because of Matthew and the cult."

Abby looked at her little sister but didn't speak. Emily could tell that Abby was letting Emily think things through before adding her own two cents.

"He has a faith, I believe," Emily continued. "But he's mad at God."

Abby smiled wistfully. "Been there, done that," she said. "When Paige died …"

She trailed off. Abby and Emily continued looking at each other in silence, and then, at the same time, each leaned toward the other for a hug.

"I know," Emily said against her sister's shoulder. "I'm trying to share with Daniel how I worked through it with God. I mean you never totally 'work through it,' but you do get to a kind of peace."

"'In the world you face persecution,'" Abby said, quoting Romans 16:33 while still wrapped in her sister's arms, "'but take heart …'"

"'I have conquered the world!'" both sisters finished together.

Emily gently pulled out of the hug but kept holding Abby's hands. "Daniel is hurting," Emily explained. "For himself and for his family. He needs God now more than ever. He has good Christian friends around him. And I think God may have brought me back into his life for that, too."

Abby took a deep breath. "OK, but don't try to be his savior," Abby advised. "That's God's job."

Emily nodded. "I know. But don't worry. He's giving as much to this friendship as I am. It's really special. We'll just see where it goes."

# CHAPTER FIFTEEN

E ach of the four weekends in December, the inn hosted a holiday dance, and as the chief organizer of events this year, Emily altered the theme each week: Dickens Christmas, old-fashioned Christmas, "Let It Snow," and wintertime in the city. The weekend activities were hits, and Emily was thrilled. There were a few glitches such as fake snow floating into the heating ducts and then being blown onto people's clothing, but it was a jolly time of year and the guests—and the other staff members—were forgiving.

In addition, for years, the inn had offered a big two-night package for New Year's Eve, and the Garretts let Emily handle all the logistics this year. Kim and Milt Garrett told her that it freed them up to focus on marketing and business planning, but Emily figured it was mostly because they knew she would love doing it. She excelled at her work, and they liked making her happy. Their two grown sons lived out of state, so they enjoyed treating her as the daughter they never had.

All the holiday activity invigorated Emily, but by the second week of January, she was exhausted. Talking to Daniel regularly became her way of catching her breath.

Since their trip to New York, Daniel and Emily had been texting fairly often, and now that the new year had passed and Emily had gotten a new laptop for Christmas that was less glitchy than her last, they had begun having virtual face-to-face chats. Talking with and seeing each other on the screen let them say a lot more than they could in texts. Emily enjoyed their conversations. As the weeks went by, she learned all about his job and his busy social schedule, which was often tied to dealing with business clients. She also learned about his friends, and she was pleased to hear him acknowledge that the faith that Paul and Marissa had was enviable.

On the surface, Emily tried to convince herself that she was just catching up with an old friend. But as each day passed, she found herself looking forward more and more to their evening talks. Even when she was working night shift, she took her break to call him.

Recently, she had even admitted to Suzie that, yes, Daniel really was attractive and funny and charming. More than that, though, he had a big heart. He was fiercely loyal to his family and, she was beginning to experience for herself, his friends. She could understand why Daniel's brother Matthew's rejection of family gatherings, which were tied to many holidays that Matthew's cult scorned, really hurt Daniel. When Matthew refused yet again to come to any family dinners over Christmastime—especially now that he had two children—Emily could see that Daniel had taken it especially hard this season.

In addition, Emily discovered that community service was important to Daniel. His job kept him really busy, but he carved out time one Saturday a month to work for Habitat for Humanity, an activity he had been involved since during college.

With all these new "observations" about Daniel, Emily had begun recognizing those butterflies in the stomach when she talked with him. The flutters had started small, but she now recognized them as similar to the ones she had when they were kids at the shore and Daniel would deign to talk with her or sit by her or play a game with her. She remembered the year he had a broken arm. He was already in high school and she was still in middle school, but because his activity was limited, he spent more time with her than usual that year. They played double solitaire at the kitchen table or read side by side on a big, puffy shore-house sofa. Daniel could still swim if he wrapped his cast in plastic, and Emily had helped him get ready for the beach every time. His hair was long that summer, and as he watched her wrap his arm, his head would be bent, and sometimes, the soft ends of that shiny, thick, brown-blonde hair would tickle her own arms. And when his head was lowered like that, she could take peeks at other parts of him, like his tanned neck and his broadening shoulders, which, to her 12-year-old mind, all worked together to make him seem very grown up. She had been beside herself with joy at the time they got to spend together that year. She bored her sisters and brother talking about it for weeks afterward.

She was beginning to feel that way again.

Daniel had begun to realize that things were changing for him, as well. He, too, was enjoying these recent, nearly nightly catchups with Emily. He felt honored that she had begun bouncing ideas off him when she planned her inn activities. And he appreciated that she let him complain about how time-consuming work had become for him. He had stopped getting uncomfortable when she mentioned church. Her faith dominated her life, but she didn't push him. She seemed to recognize that this was a subject he simply didn't really want to talk much about. And he could tell how important it was to her; he lived vicariously through the joy he heard in her voice when she talked about choir practices or chaperoning youth activities.

Within the past few weeks, he had begun to realize that he hadn't dated anyone since the fall. He assumed it was because he was extremely busy at work, but when he was really tired and let his guard down, he would admit to himself that he didn't want to hang out with any other woman besides Emily. She was sweet and nice and fun to talk with. The fact that she was beautiful, with her long, slim body, piercing blue eyes, and silky blonde hair, didn't hurt.

He would have been content to keep these new confusing feelings to himself and maybe even ignore them, but he was starting to think about her a lot more often than before. Plus, his friends had begun to notice his changing attitude. Recently, a bunch of them had been at the gym late. Because he knew he was going to miss his nightly call with Emily, Daniel had texted her to tell her that he wouldn't be home at their usual Skype time. Emily suggested that they might as well skip the call and catch up the next night. A little disappointed that she wasn't going to wait up for him, Daniel wasn't in the best mood, and his eagle-eyed friends called him on it.

"Why are you so surly tonight?" Paul asked.

"He's missing his nightly check-in with the ball and chain," Jose teased.

Jose's girlfriend, Maddie, had begun working out with them lately, and she swatted the back of her boyfriend's head. "Jose, seriously. You are a chauvinist animal."

Jose cringed. "Not you, sweetheart." Daniel watched as Jose tried to pull her in to him as she backed away, arms crossed. "You and I have an equal, loving relationship." His eyes twinkled mischievously when he turned back to Daniel. "Daniel here is simply pining for a girl he doesn't have."

"Perhaps a girl he *can't* have," Paul ventured, smiling wickedly.

"Shut up," Daniel said. "We're friends." But Paul and Jose had touched a nerve. Daniel really did care about her, and maybe he cared more than he was willing to admit. However, a relationship with Emily wasn't something he was sure he wanted to pursue. In fact, he got a sick feeling in his stomach thinking that it would really kill him if he lost her friendship by trying to take things to the next level romantically.

Maddie tapped him on the shoulder, and Daniel realized that he had been lost in his thoughts. "Just be kind to Emily," Maddie advised. And she walked across the aisle in the gym from the weights area to the EFX machines.

The next evening, when Daniel and Emily began their call, Daniel determined to be more removed. He figured he could still be kind while being distant at the same time, right? And maybe that was a better relationship to have with her. However, Emily seemed quieter than usual and a bit distracted, so he quickly scrubbed his plans and asked her if everything was all right.

"You seem subdued tonight," he observed.

"Oh, sorry," Emily responded quietly, looking down and away from her laptop camera. "It's just that it's Paige's birthday today."

Daniel gasped. "I am really sorry."

"Thank you." Emily sighed. "It's bittersweet. I remember past birthdays and fun times we had, which is great, but then I know that we'll never have those again."

"I'm so sorry," Daniel repeated. "That stinks."

Emily sighed again and looked up to face the screen. Her blue eyes were watery, and they really did look like the poets' lipid pools. Daniel longed to hug her.

"I wish I knew what to say." Daniel echoed Emily's sigh with his own.

"It's OK. I really appreciate your asking," Emily replied. She smiled slightly. Then she straightened her shoulders. "You know, Daniel, I really do know what you're going through with God. When Paige was killed, I couldn't believe that God could have let that happen. I was strong enough in my faith to know that God didn't *cause* the accident, but He could have prevented it. Paige was a geriatric nurse. She helped old people. She was good and sweet and, seriously, one of the best of all of us. Why would God want her *not* to be in this world?"

Emily paused. Daniel could hear that her voice had started to rise and maybe even crack a little, and she took a shuddering breath, which he realized was meant to calm herself.

"The sermon at the funeral helped," she continued more quietly. "The pastor knew our family well. He talked about what a loss it was. But he said too that he was frustrated by all the pat answers people give when a young person dies: 'It was God's will.' 'God needed another angel.' 'God wanted her in heaven.' He reminded us of Romans 8:22: 'We know that the whole creation has been groaning in labor pains until now.' *All creation*. It's not just people who aren't right with God, but it's also rain and trees and roads, like the accident that killed Paige. Although the kingdom is coming, the world is still not all *right* with God."

Emily shook her head quickly, as if shaking off a bad thought, and then continued: "We live in a sinful world. We can only try to remain in the Lord and trust that God knows what's best. It's definitely not easy to do."

Daniel stared at her. He ached to understand God as Emily did. She was in pain, but she was able to find comfort in God through it all. He marveled at that.

Even though Daniel knew this conversation should be about Emily and her grief, he said, "Keep praying for me." The computer microphone barely picked up his whisper.

Emily's familiar broad grin returned. "Always," she promised.

# CHAPTER SIXTEEN

Because Daniel had planned his big ski trip way back in the summer, for months it seemed as if the weekend would never arrive. But now, three days before he had to leave, he felt totally unprepared. The past two weeks, he'd been working long hours at the office to handle changes in a client's portfolio, and he hadn't had time to get organized for his trip. On his walk home from work today, Tuesday, he had learned that the snowstorm expected for the upcoming weekend was now forecasted to be much stronger than before; thus, he really wanted to start getting ready tonight.

Three friends from his firm would be going with him, and Emily had set aside a suite on the third floor of Sweet Fern Inn for the four men. Daniel would be rooming with Jerry and Jon, who had skied with him the past two winters, as well as with Ryan, the new guy from the office who was joining them for the first time. In past years, Paul had been their fourth skier, but Daniel's good buddy couldn't make the trip this year.

And Emily would be part of the vacation as well. She and her neighbor, Suzie, had taken a few vacation days to ski with them and also planned to stay the whole time at the inn, in a room on the first floor. Thinking about Emily and vacation reminded Daniel of all those years at the shore. He smiled at the thought of how he'd mostly just tolerated her when they were young. He was never cruel to her—his father and mother would not have allowed it—but he did openly try to avoid her when she got too close to him. Truthfully, deep down, he often thought she was kind-of fun and daring for a little kid, but he never wanted the older kids to know he felt that way.

For some reason, thinking about Emily and vacation also unnerved him now as he began preparing for the ski trip. Well, he actually did know the reason. He clearly was attracted to Emily. He had been toying with making this weekend a time to let her know. As he had often done before, he had wrestled with himself over the possible loss of their strengthening friendship if she said she wasn't interested, but he finally had decided that it was worth the risk. Having her this close would force his hand, which was probably a good thing. In his mushiest moments, which he tried to avoid, he admitted that he liked so many things about her: her honest eyes, her lilting laugh, her dedication to her job, her concern for others. And she kept him on his toes, which was a selfish reason to like her, but it was what it was.

He shook off his thoughts and threw his big maroon duffel bag on the bed and opened it, and then he sent a group text to the other three men: *Storm coming. Bring extra layers. We'll either have great conditions or be snowed in.*

Next, Daniel went into his guest bedroom and opened the lid to his late grandmother's cedar chest. When he was in his teens, Grandmom Mac loved hearing him regale her with all the silly details of his ski adventures, and when she died and left him the chest, he felt he could honor her best by storing all his ski clothes there. For this weekend, he figured there'd be a need for at least four days of ski garb, so he grabbed four thermal shirts and matching pants and threw them on the floor beside him. Not everyone had such a large wardrobe just for skiing, but he had learned years ago that it skeeved him out to wear the same long underwear in one weekend if there were no washing machines around. Land's End and Winter Silks kept him wardrobed. He grabbed four hats, six pairs of socks, and his favorite gloves along with two other pair—just in case.

His ski boots stood beside the chest, and he picked them up by their joined laces, towered the clothes on top of his folded arms, and carried them all to his own bedroom. He was a planner: he liked to be packed a few days ahead of time so that he could add things over the next few days as he remembered them. He dumped the piled clothes on top of the open duffel and took a breath.

Just then, his computer pinged, and he tapped a key and smiled to see Emily's lovely face on his screen.

"Oh, my goodness," she exclaimed, looking past him to the big duffel bag covered with the mountain of clothes on his bed. "Are you planning to move here?"

"Ha, ha, ha," he said, enunciating each ha. "All my clothes are bigger than yours. And I bet you're not even packed at all yet, right?"

"I live 10 minutes away from the hotel." Emily laughed. "I can come back if I forget anything. Too bad we're not the same size; I'd lend you something if you needed it."

The thought of borrowing an item of clothing from Emily made Daniel's cheeks hot, and he brought his hand up to scratch his forehead in order to hide his face from the laptop camera.

"I think the conditions will be fantastic with all the snow we're expecting," Daniel said quickly.

Emily took Daniel's change of topic in stride and looked thoughtful. "It's actually supposed to be a pretty big storm. I hope we don't lose electricity. Using the generator takes its toll on the inn."

"I'm sure it will be fine, but if not, I refuse to let a little darkness dampen my mood," Daniel declared. "Anyway, I usually only get to take this one trip a year, so I try to spend as much time as possible on the slopes."

Emily brightened. "It's going to be mongo fun!" Her cat suddenly appeared and pushed his furry brown head against the computer, blocking out Emily's face. Daniel heard her laugh lightly and gently pushed him aside.

"Big Boy!" she admonished. When the cat finally moved, leaving his tail on the keyboard, Emily continued. "Tell me about your friends who are coming."

Daniel didn't like the small pang of jealousy he felt when she asked about the other guys in his group. He had already told his friends that they were not allowed to pursue her, despite how sexist that had sounded. Of course, he didn't tell them about his own interest in her, but he indicated that she was an old family friend and that she was to remain off-limits.

Internally shaking his head of those thoughts, Daniel explained to Emily that Jerry and Jon had started at the firm the same time he did. They were around the same age and had similar hobbies, and this would be their third year skiing the Poconos together. Ryan was new to their group. He worked in a different department, but he was also about their age and had really shown an interest in their ski trip the day he started at their office a few months earlier.

"I don't know him that well," Daniel admitted. "But he seems nice enough, and we'll be skiing most of the time anyway. We don't have to be best friends or anything."

"Is he cute?" Emily asked.

Again, Daniel felt that stab of jealousy. He didn't answer immediately.

Emily giggled. "I'm always trying to find a good man for Suzie."

"I guess he's OK." Daniel hoped it wasn't too obvious that he felt this relieved. "I'm a guy; I can't tell."

"Well, I gotta go to work tonight, and I probably should at least think about packing," Emily concluded. "So I'll let you get back to your mound of clothes. I'll see you Thursday night."

After Emily clicked off, she was a bit surprised at how excited she was. She lived in the Poconos; she could ski whenever she wanted. Thus, although having a full long weekend off from work to ski was a bit of a luxury, the idea of hanging with friends on the slopes was not new for her. But this was going to be a whole weekend with Daniel, who was smart and funny and gorgeous and fast becoming a person that she wanted to spend way more time with. To that extent, this weekend was special.

Emily gasped. She suddenly remembered that the one "special" thing she was supposed to be doing this past week was take care of

Chloe. She had been responsible up until then and had taken her neighbor dog for a walk twice already that day, but she realized that Chloe needed one more trek around the block before Emily left for work. Chloe's owners would be arriving back home on late Thursday night, when Emily left to ski.

"Hey, girl," Emily called as she entered her neighbors' living room. The big yellow dog ran across the floor and slid to a stop in front of her. Chloe gave a single happy bark, and her fluffy tail knocked the mail off the end table where Emily had just laid it. Emily laughed, replaced the envelopes and flyers on the table, clipped on Chloe's leash, and led the dog to the backyard. It was oppressively dark outside, with no moon, so a walk around the block on the poorly paved country roads was out of the question. But the Jenners had a two-acre backyard, and Emily could let Chloe inspect all corners of the yard as they walked the perimeter. She pulled out of her down-jacket pocket the small flashlight she had carried from home and flicked it on. In winter, not only was it eerily dark at the Jenners, but it was eerily quiet as well. Living in an apartment, Emily was used to the shuffle of feet in the hallway and the gentle closing of apartment doors. Even nights at the inn were not as still as this. She shivered.

"Chloe, I don't think we're going all the way to the end of the yard tonight." Emily stroked the dog's side. "It's spooky out here."

As if to support Emily's fear, Chloe's head shot up and the dog stared into the darkness to the left. Chloe pulled Emily to the edge of a row of tall evergreens that marked the one side of the Jenner's property. Emily stopped and listened. She, too, heard the rustling. She waited.

Finally, she ventured a quiet, "Hello, is anyone there?"

The rustling stopped. Emily and Chloe stood still for what seemed like many minutes, and finally Emily patted the dog's head. "Come on, it was probably a bird. Let's keep walking."

About 15 minutes later, when they returned and neared the same spot, Chloe pulled again on the leash to go toward the trees where they had earlier heard the noise. Not wanting to revisit her fear, Emily wound the leash several times around her hand, which brought Chloe closer and closer until the big yellow Labrador was right beside her. Again, Emily pet the dog's fur. "Let's go in, Chloe," Emily urged. "All this darkness and quietness is making us both imagine things!"

When they got back into the house, Emily prayed out loud: "Sorry, God, for being afraid. That was silly to be so scared. I know you teach me to be wary, but I also know you're watching over Chloe and me."

The Lab's ears perked up at her name. Emily tousled the short fur on the dog's head. "Here's a treat." She handed a bone-shaped snack to Chloe who had patiently sat at attention. "You were brave out there. I'm off to work, where I recognize what all those sounds are!"

# CHAPTER SEVENTEEN

"You do know that Brandon is coming this weekend with his girlfriend," Kim Garrett pointed out as she and Emily were finishing up some paperwork together in the office. The two women were seated back to back. Kim sat in front of a screen at the large desk, and Emily had her laptop on the long table behind the desk.

"Yeah." Emily swiveled her chair to face Kim's. "I don't mean to come across as catty, but I thought it was interesting that he booked just one room for the two of them."

"Are you upset?" Kim, too, turned her chair.

Emily smiled wistfully. "Not really. After I broke up with Brandon, I realized that although I cared for him, there really wasn't a future there. I think he and I are a lot more different than I realized. I mean, he's a really nice guy. He is. In fact, I wish we could have stayed friends, but sadly, that was not to be."

"Hmm." Kim raised her eyes thoughtfully toward the ceiling.

"What?"

"Did you know that the hotel chain he works for is trying to buy Sweet Fern?" Kim asked, dropping her eyes to meet Emily's gaze.

Emily's jaw dropped. "What?" she repeated.

Kim sighed, her creamy brown face in a scowl. "That big conglomerate wants this land. Of course, Sweet Fern is doing well as an independent inn, but it's not as if we're a runaway success. They could knock the place down and build a much bigger hotel that would attract more people and make more money."

"But the size and the charm are what sell this place!" Emily turned her chair in a circle, arms wide, to indicate the whole of the inn.

"I know," Kim agreed. "But boy, with the things that have been happening lately, such as the boiler breaking and new shingles needed in a couple of places, I sometimes wonder if a group with deeper pockets could do better."

"Ugh," Emily groaned. "'Do better'? It would just be another cookie-cutter place to stay. No way!"

Kim took a deep, worried breath. "But a place like this is dependent on its loyal clientele, and that can be a bad thing. Did you know that half of our reservations for this weekend have been canceled? People don't want to get stuck here in a snowstorm."

"We'll make it up next weekend." Emily clapped a hand on the older woman's shoulder. "There will be great snow for skiing then, right?"

"Of course," Kim affirmed, brightening slightly. "Well, we're not down and out yet anyway. I'm still headed to Orlando this weekend for that small-hotel-owners conference. I guess fewer guests means it will be easier for my hubby to take care of the inn by himself."

Emily chuckled. "I know I'm officially off, but Milt knows he can call me if he needs me, right?"

Kim nodded, and the two turned their chairs and went back to their respective papers and computers, working in comfortable silence. Emily said a quick prayer: *Dear God, please let this be a profitable season for the Garretts. They work amazingly hard, and I love this inn.*

"Hey," Emily said as she moved a piece of paper from her to-do work pile to her finished pile, "did you know that a guy called last week and asked about the Grace Kelly rumor?"

Kim looked over her shoulder at Emily, smiled, and rolled her eyes. "Well, the princess *did* stay here once."

"No, I mean the rumor that one of her attendants stole Grace's jewels and hid them in the floorboards."

Kim let out a full laugh this time and then continued the myth: "And the man was arrested for another theft before he could come back and retrieve them."

Emily shrugged, returning the smile.

"Well, we've redone just about all the floors in this inn over the years," Kim explained. "No jewels." She closed her eyes and shuddered. "But lots of disgusting dead flies and other bugs with too many legs, and grimy, smelly candy wrappers! Ick."

Emily patted her friend's shoulder sympathetically Then she printed out the last spreadsheet she was working on, put the printout into her folder, and closed it. As she stood, her phone pinged. It was Daniel.

*Ready for the snow?*

She laughed and replied, *Can't wait.*

"Is that Daniel?" Kim asked.

Emily nodded.

"He seems like a great guy," Kim said with a lilt that implied, "He'd be great for you!"

"I know, I know." Emily felt a slight warmth on her cheeks. "I think he and I need to talk this weekend about where our friendship is headed. I thought I just liked him as a friend, but the more we talk, the more I'm beginning to feel more than that."

Kim lifted a shoulder. "You're usually good at direct conversations."

"Oh, I've always thought game-playing was silly." Emily waved one hand to shoo away the idea of not being truthful. "Of course, my 'directness' isn't always appreciated. Just last week, my sister Abby called me Emily Blunt—you know, the actress. But she didn't mean that as a compliment. Being a hospitality management major has helped, though. I've had to learn about filtering what I really want to say."

"OK, then, are you going to drop the filters now and tell Daniel how you feel?" Kim asked.

Emily put her hand on her chin as she thought. "I'm not exactly sure how to do that as an adult," she admitted. "When I was a kid, I'd just tackle him!" She shook her head and chuckled.

"Your eyes sparkle when you talk about him."

Emily knew she was blushing a full-on red this time. "I'll be honest. I don't know if he's even interested in me like that. We talk all the time, and it's obvious he cares about me. But he's busy with work, and he's such a city boy. I kind of think he sees me as a little sister living in the woods."

"Can't hurt to test that," Kim said, wiggling her eyebrows.

Emily laughed. "We'll see."

# CHAPTER EIGHTEEN

As at least three of them had done every year for the past three years, Daniel and his friends impressed themselves with being able to fit four men plus their suitcases and duffels into Jerry's Buick Encore. Daniel called shotgun, and he was able to doze on and off during the two hours it took to get to the Poconos. As soon as Jerry pulled the SUV around the corner into the side parking lot of the inn, Daniel shimmied to sit up straight. When he did, he saw Emily standing in front of the quaint building's sliding lobby doors, rubbing her arms and hopping up and down. She was wearing a hat but no coat.

"You're early!" Emily squealed as she ran to meet them when they parked. "From inside, I could see the skis on top of the car, and I figured it must be you guys."

"We had no traffic." Daniel stepped out of the car and hugged her briefly. Then he patted her head as he pulled back to survey her. "Nice hat, but you don't have a jacket on! You look like you're freezing."

"I'm fine, but hurry up," Emily said, this time rubbing her legs, which were covered in what looked like light denim. "I hate to be cold." She followed Daniel as he walked around to open the back hatch.

"They're all afraid of a little snow!" Daniel's friend Jon had stepped out of the vehicle, as had the other men, and was walking toward Emily, arms outstretched. Daniel could have sworn his best friend's nearly black eyes sparkled with flirtation in his dark brown face as he flashed a brilliant smile. "Hey, I'm Jon. Do I get a hug too?"

Emily embraced him and then hugged the other two men who each introduced themselves and insisted on a hug as greeting as well.

Daniel frowned at the twinges of jealousy he felt at the attention Emily was giving the other men, and he tried to shake off those feelings. He was sure these guys weren't Emily's type. Then again, what *was* Emily's type? Did Emily think of *him* as her type? He definitely planned to say something this weekend about his growing interest in her, but he still wasn't exactly sure what it was he felt for her or how strong those feelings were.

Someone slapped the back of his head, and Daniel realized that he was staring into the back of the SUV. "Are you still sleeping?" Jerry asked. Jerry was the jokester of the group, and his smile always seemed to go from his lips to the tips of his freckles and dark red hair. He turned to address Emily. "Daniel snored the whole way here."

Daniel glared at Jerry and then moved away, ducking his head to avoid another slap. He jerked his duffel and ski boots out of the back of the SUV, turned, and nearly knocked Emily over. He dropped his bag and caught her arm before she fell.

She looked beautiful. Her hat was a white, wool, knitted cap pulled low on her head, and blonde strands peeked out from the bottom edges to curl around her neck. Her royal-blue, cable-knit turtleneck accented her eyes, and her cheeks were already pink from the cold.

Nope, he didn't need to wonder what he felt for Emily. He was a goner.

"Suzie will be up in about an hour," Emily was saying, as she took Daniel's ski boots from his hand and peeked into the storage section of the SUV looking for more things to help carry.

"Another lovely lady is joining us?" Jerry asked, both eyebrows raised. "I'm gonna love this weekend!"

It was Daniel's turn to slap a head. "We're here to ski, not fall in love," he reprimanded. Of course, he wasn't so sure about that for himself.

"Tsk, tsk," Emily was shaking her head in mock chastisement. "We're all skiing and hanging out and it's going to be great!"

Emily smiled, enjoying the men's banter. She was still a little surprised at how excited she felt, and she was pretty sure that her renewed attraction to Daniel was at least part of the reason for her excitement. She grabbed Daniel's elbow to pull him closer, ostensibly so that she could whisper in his ear, but she knew it was just nice to have the chance to touch him. His neck smelled good, a little spicy, and she momentarily forgot what she was going to say. Before she could open her mouth, his hair tickled her nose, which made her turn her head and sneeze. Daniel backed away to look at her, concerned. "God bless you." The others echoed the blessing.

She laughed and leaned forward again but spoke in a stage whisper in order that all could hear: "I was going to say that I want you to keep your eye on these guys this weekend. No funny business."

"They're all bark, no bite," Daniel assured her as the others walked inside the inn ahead of them and missed the rest of Daniel and Emily's conversation. "Actually, I don't really know Ryan. He's kind of quiet. But I think he's harmless. He doesn't talk much about girls or hobbies or anything." He tilted his head, obviously considering something. "He talks mostly about money, which is weird since that's our job and that's the last thing I want to talk about when I'm not working!"

The men headed upstairs to their room to unpack, while Emily went to her own room right down the hall from the main lobby. Suzie arrived shortly before 6, and Emily helped her settle into what would be their shared home for the next few days. They chatted for a bit and then left and walked to meet Daniel and his friends in the restaurant on the same floor.

The dining room was nearly empty. A mother, father, and two elementary-school-age boys sat near the entryway to the restaurant. A young man and woman sat huddled together in a corner table with their backs to the room. Daniel's crew had pushed together two four-person tables in the middle of the restaurant and had already been served drinks. Jon, Jerry, and Ryan each had beers, and Emily was pleased to see that Daniel was drinking what looked like iced tea.

Suzie had noticed Daniel's drink as well. "A teetotaler?" Emily's friend asked as she approached the table and moved to sit next to Daniel.

Daniel rose politely as Suzie sat. "Just keeping these guys honest. If one of us is sober, that should keep the others from falling into debauchery!"

"Great word!" Emily said as she sat down across from Daniel. He had stayed standing until she got comfortable.

"What a gallant," Jon said. "You didn't give any time for the rest of us to stand like gentlemen, too."

"You were glued to the menu." Jerry poked a finger at the paper in Jon's hands. "Food before manners for us, I'd say."

Emily's eyes met Suzie's and they smiled, both recognizing the easy camaraderie of the friends.

Seated next to her, Jon leaned close to Emily and said, "There's no curry on this menu."

A quick flush stung Emily's face. "We, uh, don't have much variety up here, um, in the Poconos."

"Jon." Daniel lightly punched his friend in the arm, chastising, and then turned to Emily. "He told me once that he doesn't even like curry!"

"Not the way you Americans do it!"

"You were born in America, Jon!" Daniel said. "You *are* American."

Jon huffed and winked at Emily. Daniel felt that Green Monster thing again—this time, a bit stronger. He didn't like it.

"Who cares?" Jerry whined. "I'm starved. Let's eat!"

# CHAPTER NINETEEN

Emily could tell that Mike, the waiter, recognized Daniel from his first visit to the inn. Daniel greeted him and introduced his friends. They all chatted a bit about the storm predictions, but then they quickly got down to the business of placing their orders.

After Mike left, Suzie looked past Daniel to the quiet young man at the other end of the table. "So, Ryan, I hear you're new to this gang. How long have you worked with these guys?"

"Not long," Ryan answered. "But as soon as I found out that they were coming to this inn, I had to get myself invited."

The rest of the group turned to look at Ryan. "Why?" Daniel asked, voicing the joint question of the group.

Ryan looked uneasy, but he gulped and replied, "I heard about the Grace Kelly jewels, and that story interests me." He glanced hopefully toward Emily. "Is it true that they are hidden here somewhere?"

"Not according to these second-generation owners," Emily said. "A man actually called about that last week, and I asked my boss. Kim is one of the owners. She laughed so hard that I had trouble even getting an answer out of her. She says that she has no idea how that rumor started and that, with all the renovations over the years, there's no way anything valuable could be hidden here."

Ryan scowled. "Well, I don't think it's funny. There are a lot of good hiding nooks in a place like this inn."

"Ha! Those jewels are the only things that could help this inn." The harsh voice behind her startled Emily, and she looked up to see her ex-boyfriend, Brandon, and a young woman standing behind her chair. The woman had long wavy black hair that spilled down the front of her low-cut dress. She looked as if she were ready for an evening at a nightclub instead of dinner at a small Pocono inn. Brandon was wearing a suit. Emily realized that they had been the couple in the corner of the restaurant.

"Brandon!" Emily started to jump up, wanting to hug him in greeting, but she quickly sensed his animosity and decided to just extend her hand from where she sat.

"Hello, Emily," Brandon said coolly, reaching to touch her hand and then just as quickly letting it go. "I think you've met Karen, the general manager of the Harris Consortium of Hotels in Philadelphia."

Emily began again to stand up, but Karen waved her back down.

"Please don't get up," Karen said. "We just came to your table to say hello. Brandon, let's not bother them."

Brandon snorted. "I don't think Perfect Emily can get bothered."

Emily's mouth dropped, and she felt her whole body grow hot with embarrassment and then anger—at both Brandon for what he said and herself for the way she was feeling. She was sure her face looked like a tomato ripening in front of everyone.

Daniel jumped up and reached his hand across the table. "Nice meeting you then, Karen," he said. Karen politely shook his hand. He grabbed Brandon's hand as well before the other man could react. "Good to see you again, Brandon." Daniel shook Brandon's hand heartily, dropped it, and then sat as quickly as he had stood up, clearly signaling an end to the conversation.

Suzie touched Emily's knee under the table and said kindly, "Let's check out the ladies' room."

The two women excused themselves, while Brandon and Karen went back to their table.

In the rest room, Emily splashed water on her face and then looked in the mirror. "How could he say that to me—call me Perfect Emily? First, he says something awful about the inn, and then he insults me —in front of my friends."

She grabbed a paper towel and whirled toward Suzie. "Do I act like I think I'm perfect, Suzie? I would hate for people to see me that way."

"No," Suzie assured her. "Besides, you're dripping water all over, and that's not a perfect thing to do." Smiling, Suzie took the paper towel from Emily's clenched hands and began gently wiping her friend's face. "You're nice, and some people aren't used to others being nice to them."

"But Brandon sees me as a snob!"

"He's just mad because you're the one who broke up with him," Suzie soothed. "Besides, you've got a much better, much more hand-some man interested in you. Focus on that."

Emily felt her cheeks go pink again. She started to open her mouth to protest, but she shut it without comment. Suzie just tilted her head and grinned. Smiling back sheepishly, Emily gave a little shrug and scrunched up her nose. "I do kind of like Daniel."

"*He's* your future," Susie declared, "not Brandon." She threw the paper towel away and handed Emily a fresh one.

"You're a good friend."

The women walked back to the table, and as Emily sat, she noticed Daniel glaring at Brandon. She got a little thrill to know that Daniel was feeling angry for her. As she settled into her seat, she touched his hand, and he turned to her, a scowl left over on his face. She smiled an "I'm OK" smile, and he nodded, understanding.

"Now, isn't the bread amazing?" Emily asked, picking up a soft, warm piece from the recently delivered basket.

Jon leaned to her and, with a furrowed brow but that same bright smile, asked, "You knew that guy, Emily?" He motioned with his head toward where Brandon and Karen were sitting. "And you're also friends with Daniel here? Sheesh, you should choose better friends!"

Then he put his arm around her shoulders, made sure he caught her gaze, and winked. "You're a good egg, Emily."

Their food arrived, and Brandon and Karen were soon forgotten. The six of them ate, chatted, and laughed for the next three hours. At one point, Emily leaned over to Suzie and whispered, "I think we're fitting in. I don't think they'll ditch us on the slopes." Suzie's shoulders shook in quiet laughter.

After dinner, the six of them drifted from the restaurant to the elevators.

"I'll never be able to ski tomorrow," Jerry groaned, sticking out his stomach and patting it. "I've gained 20 pounds from dinner."

"You're a nut!" Daniel shook his head and pressed the up arrow on the elevator. The rest of the group laughed.

"We'll see you all tomorrow," Emily said, still laughing. She looped her arm through Suzie's and began steering her friend down the hall toward their room.

"8 a.m. dressed and in the lobby," Daniel called to the women as the elevator doors opened and the men stepped in.

Back in the room, the women each plopped on one of the single beds.

"I ate too much too," Suzie commented. "I should be getting stuff ready for tomorrow, but now I can't move."

Emily chuckled an agreement.

"Hey." Suzie leaned up on one elbow to face her friend, "Daniel is amazing. He's generous and kind and smart and funny. And that bit with Brandon? He protected you like a fierce silverback."

"A silverback? Seriously?"

Suzie shrugged. "I saw a PBS special on gorillas this weekend. What can I say? Anyway, do you think he'll make a move this weekend?"

"I'm not sure what that would look like," Emily admitted, lying on her back and staring at the ceiling. She stayed that way for a minute and then sat up and blurted, "I do like him. I'm not sure what to do about that. Do I, like, ask him on a date or what? Do I wait for him to tell me how he feels? Do I tell him first? This is silly; I'm an adult."

Suzie puffed out a laugh and dropped her head back on the three fluffy white pillows piled at the top of her bed. "You're overthinking it."

"Ha, you don't know the half of it," Emily moaned. "I'm not sure if there are 'rules' from a Christian dating point of view. I mean, I want to be with a Christian man …"

Suzie sat up and grew serious. She swung her legs in the space between the two beds. "Emily, you said that Daniel is searching. He has Christian family and friends, and he respects your faith. God is clearly working in him, right?"

Emily nodded.

"Then let God take this relationship and run with it." Suzie grabbed both of her friend's hands, squeezed them, and held on. "Jesus, please guide Emily as she grows closer to Daniel. Show him your way, and help the two of them search for your will together."

Emily looked up, feeling the tears starting to pool in her eyes. "Suzie, you are seriously the best friend ever."

Suzie smiled. "You're welcome. Now let's get our ski stuff ready for tomorrow. Daniel seemed pretty fierce about that 8 a.m. meet-up time!"

# CHAPTER TWENTY

I n the morning, the two women were already waiting in the lobby when the men lugged their ski equipment off the elevator to meet them. Ever the organized one, Emily handed Daniel a take-out carton with three coffees for the road, plus two paper bags.

Nodding to the bags, she said, "Egg sandwiches from the breakfast chef. Suzie and I already put our to-go food in Suzie's car, along with our ski stuff."

Jerry grabbed a coffee from the container Daniel was holding and asked, "Can you come home with us and take care of us every day?"

"Yeah," Jon agreed, grabbing another of the coffees from the container. "You have got to find a way to convince her to marry you *now*, Daniel!"

Daniel chuckled awkwardly and stole a glance at Emily. She smiled, unconcerned. Then she shook her head, shrugged, and announced, "Let's hit the road."

Conditions at Winter Wonderland were perfect. In fact, Daniel decided it was some of the best skiing he ever remembered having. Pocono slopes tended to be icy and rough on the skis. Most skiers from the area joked that if you could ski the Pocono Mountains, you could ski anywhere. Daniel once told a client from Vermont that

Pocono skiing was more like sliding around on two thin logs in a tilted icy pond than actual downhill skiing. But today, the snow had started early in the morning and continued throughout the day, giving them fresh, thick powder to slice through all morning and afternoon. The ground was soft but supportive, with no icy or mushy patches, and the slopes were white and wide and gorgeous.

All day, the falling snow was steady but light, and there was no wind. And with temperatures right at the freezing mark, the air wasn't too cold.

In addition, with threat of a storm, many potential skiers had chosen to stay at home, so even for a Friday, the slopes were fairly clear of people.

Daniel, Emily, and their friends began skiing when Winter Wonderland opened, and they took only two breaks, one for lunch and one to warm up in the afternoon. They had planned to leave at 4 in the afternoon to get back to the inn and cleaned up in time for dinner.

Emily wasn't as good a skier as he was, but Daniel stayed on the intermediate slopes, the blue squares, most of the day with her, Suzie, and Ryan. He took a few runs down the double diamond slopes, but most of those led to the bottom of the same ski lifts as those for the blue squares, so he would wait after a run for the others to catch up. In addition to being able to spend time with Emily, Daniel also thought this would be a good time to get to know the new guy better. However, Ryan remained quiet throughout the day, even when Daniel rode up with him alone on the two-seater chairlifts.

Of course, Daniel was just being polite when he offered to ride with Ryan on occasion. Most of the time, all four of them took the quad lifts, and he always jockeyed to sit beside Emily.

"How are things at work?" Daniel asked Emily during what he figured would be their last trip up the mountain. The two of them were pressed together on the bench in the middle of the chairlift between Suzie and Ryan, which Daniel didn't mind. He was wearing lightweight black ski pants, which meant he really wasn't squishing Emily. She, however, had on the thickest tan-colored snow pants he'd ever seen, under a light-blue down jacket. When he watched her on the slopes, her legs looked like one big tree trunk under a lovely sky—a really cute tree trunk at that. He was impressed that she was able to maneuver at all. Because she had, indeed, claimed that she hated being cold, he guessed he shouldn't be surprised.

He realized that he did know, of course, how things were going at Emily's work since he talked with her nearly every day. But he loved hearing her light, lilting voice struggle to make itself heard through the muffle of the bottom part of her balaclava.

"Work is great," Emily replied. "Like I told you, I'm doing more and more with the event planning, and I love it. I think I'm doing fairly well with it, too, because the event agency we use has offered to pay for me to attend a workshop in the spring. It's a good business move for them as well because that will keep the inn coming back to them for the events."

Suzie leaned around Emily to get Daniel's attention. "Emily is mighty good at that," Suzie said. "She helped organized a bunch of parties at Christmas time, and the themes and decorations were amazing. When we get back to the inn, I'll show you some pics I took of the activities."

"Suzie is such a great cheerleader," Emily claimed. "But she's amazing at her job too. She keeps getting promotions. I just don't really know what it is she does." Emily chuckled apologetically.

Suzie lightly elbowed her friend and smiled. She leaned forward, making sure that Daniel could hear her. "I'm a project manager for the IT department for Pocono Regional Medical Center. I've got good peeps, so it's easy to excel. How about you, Daniel? Emily says you're in finance."

Daniel nodded. "I'm an analyst. I have a couple of big clients, and I'm in charge of 'wooing' others. That's actually what they call it. I like my job, but I'm a bit of a workaholic, I know. I'm working on trying not to take it home with me all the time. I'm trying to make sure I have time to do more things like this."

"I hear ya," Ryan chimed in from the other side of Daniel. The other three on the lift looked to him. He shrugged. "Personally, I think the best career is being independently wealthy."

Daniel interrupted the conversation with "Bar up," and the rest of them turned forward and realized they were close to the end of their ride. Daniel raised the rail of the chairlift, and they all glided to the end of the bench and scooted off.

"Last run!" Daniel shouted behind him. He took off quickly so that he could stop halfway down the mountain at the point where the slope broke into two. That had been the habit of the lead skier—to stop to wait for the others to determine which side to ski down to finish the run. Suzie and Ryan reached Daniel first. They paused and then skied past him down the right slope. When Emily got to where Daniel was waiting, she stopped. He pulled down his green Philadelphia Eagles scarf and smiled at her. Although her face was covered, Daniel could tell that Emily was smiling back at him. Her eyes crinkled. It made his heart jump happily.

"What a day!" he exclaimed.

"I know," Emily agreed through a fleece-covered face. "I really like this."

"I really like *you*," Daniel replied quickly. Although he surprised himself at how that came out, it was close to what he had been trying to say all day. He hadn't been sure how or when to say it, but as it turned out, the words were simple and straightforward and what he meant. OK. It was now out there. He looked expectantly at Emily.

Emily didn't hesitate. "I like you too." She placed a gloved hand on his arm. With the other hand, she pulled the balaclava down from her mouth and let him see her smile this time, and he smiled back in relief.

"I do," Emily continued. "I like you. I'm so glad you said something because—"

Emily didn't get to finish as, just then, Jerry shushed to a stop behind them, spraying snow everywhere.

"Really?" Daniel asked, wiping snow from his goggles. He had been facing uphill and got the brunt of the splash.

Jerry grabbed Daniel's arm and pulled. "Let's go!" Jerry yelled.

And for now, that was the end of the conversation.

# CHAPTER TWENTY-ONE

They had taken two cars to the slopes, and Daniel was a little disappointed that, on the ride back to the inn, they took the same cars they had driven in that morning: the men all in the Encore, with Emily and Suzie in Suzie's two-door white Hyundai Elantra.

It was a slower return ride, because of the snow, and when both cars arrived back at the inn, they all stumbled through the big front doors, lugging skis, poles, and boots, more than one of them moaning with exhaustion.

"Dinner at the restaurant in an hour," Jerry called as he led the men toward the elevators, "for anyone who doesn't fall asleep before then."

"Emily!" From the front desk, Stacey called to their group, and Emily turned.

"You head in," she said to Suzie as she walked to the front desk. "I'll be there in a minute."

Daniel left the men and walked with Emily. "I'll come with you."

Emily looked up at him and grinned in thanks, but he could see other emotions flitting in her eyes as well. Perhaps she, like him, was figuring out how to continue the conversation they had started on the mountain. They had only exchanged some "I like you's," but those few words required a lot of unpacking.

At the desk, Stacey handed Emily a note while Daniel stood a few steps back, giving them privacy, although it was easy to overhear the conversation. "Your next-door neighbor called," Stacey explained. "Mrs. Jenner said she was panicking about her dog. She asked if you could watch Chloe this weekend. They were told they can't fly home in this coming storm. I think the snow already hit wherever they were planning to land."

"Thanks." Emily took the note from the young woman.

"I tried to give her your cell phone number," Stacey said apologetically, "but she asked me to have you call her back on the land-line number she gave me."

Emily laughed. "She has a cell phone but doesn't know how to use it." She waved the note at Stacey. "Thanks again."

Emily walked a few steps away from the desk and paused, studying the note.

"What's up?" Daniel asked.

"I have to get Chloe, but I'm not sure what to do with her." Emily bounced her fist against her chin. She caught herself and quickly dropped her arm, but she continued to think, this time chewing on her lower lip.

"Can't you bring her to your room here?"

Emily went back to tapping her chin. "We don't allow pets."

Stacey came around the side of the main desk and put her arm around Emily's waist. "It's a weird weekend," Stacey said. "There are hardly any people at the inn. Couldn't you just text Mr. Garrett and ask if he can make an exception for just a few days?"

"Chloe's a big dog …"

"Text him," Daniel agreed. "Or call. It can't hurt." Daniel felt sorry for the dog and for Emily. However, he had to admit that he also did not want to lose out on this ski weekend with Emily if she had to go stay at her neighbors' house because of a stranded dog.

He watched as Emily nodded, squeezed Stacey once, and moved out of the younger woman's embrace. Then, pulling out her cell phone, Emily scrolled through her contacts and pressed a number. She waited, and Daniel realized she must have gotten the owner's voice mail.

"Milt, it's Emily Steverman. Is it OK if I bring a dog to my hotel room for the weekend? Suzie and I are on the first floor, and I'll keep Chloe in the room except when I need to walk her. You've met Chloe. She's really good. Her owners can't get home because of the storm, and I think this is my only choice." Emily paused and then shrugged. "Thanks. Bye."

She hung up and returned to gnawing her lower lip.

"I need to go get her," Emily declared.

"I'll go with you," Daniel volunteered before she even finished her sentence.

Emily shook her head and started to protest, but Daniel gently took her shoulders and turned her to face him. "It's going to get worse sooner rather than later," he said. "We should both go get the dog and bring her back here. It's safer that way. We'll be together. I'm sure your Mr. Garrett will be fine with it—at least for this one night."

Emily nodded, and they agreed to meet in the lobby in ten minutes after they dropped things off in their rooms. "I'll call the Jenners and reassure them that I'm getting Chloe," Emily called back as she headed to her room.

Daniel took the stairs to the third floor and used his key to get into the men's suite. When he entered, Jon was sitting on the bed nearest the door, checking his iPad, and Ryan was at the desk on his laptop. Daniel heard the shower running in the bathroom.

"I need the keys to Jerry's Encore," Daniel announced. "Emily has to go pick up her neighbor's dog and bring it back here."

Jon grinned with a knowing look that Daniel couldn't quite comprehend. Then Jon lifted a set of keys from the nightstand between his bed and the one next to it and handed them to Daniel. "You can tell him yourself." He jerked his head toward the bathroom door.

Daniel snorted and rolled his eyes. He opened the door to the bathroom a few inches.

"Yo, Jerry."

"Ack!" Jerry cried out. Daniel heard something drop to the shower floor, probably a shampoo or soap.

"Sheesh, bro, you scared the stuffing out of me," Jerry complained.

"Sorry. I just wanted to let you know that I'm taking the keys to your Encore."

"Why?" Jerry asked, still irritated.

"I want to test it on the back roads in the snow."

"What!"

Daniel snickered. "Seriously, I need to go with Emily to pick up her neighbor's dog. The poor animal has been alone since last night, and Emily's car can't make the ride in this snow."

"Oh." There was a pause. "Sure. That seems reasonable. Just be careful. You know how I love that SUV. It's my baby. But if it's for love …" Jerry trailed off, and Daniel walked out of the bathroom, firmly—and loudly—closing the door behind him. He heard Jerry's "Ack!" again.

Before leaving the room, Daniel dug into his suitcase and pulled out a dry pair of gloves and a Phillies baseball cap. He replaced his long undershirt and sweater with a long-sleeve T-shirt. He didn't bother to take the extra time to change out of his ski pants, but he did put his down jacket back on. The year before, he had sprung for a dark-blue, lightweight Patagonia ski coat that was waterproof and weighed only a pound or two, and he was certainly glad of it now.

By the time Daniel got back down to the lobby, he saw that Emily, too, had gone to her room and not only replaced her hat and gloves but also put on a warm-looking pair of corduroys.

Emily smiled thankfully when she saw him. "Hey, I'm glad you changed, too. I felt grungy in my ski clothes, and my hat and gloves were wet."

"We don't know what it will be like by the time we start heading back here," Daniel explained. "If I have to brush off the car, I want to do it with dry extremities!"

# CHAPTER TWENTY-TWO

Driving out of the parking lot of the inn wasn't too difficult. Someone had plowed recently, and the snow coming down was still soft, so the SUV's tires were able to hold the road as Daniel slowly steered onto the main street. Once out of the protected parking lot, however, the Encore immediately began to slide. Daniel was going slow enough to control the vehicle, but Emily could tell immediately that it would be a long and white-knuckle drive. She had hoped that the two of them might be able to talk about their conversation that had been cut short on the slopes, but as soon as they turned onto the road, she knew this wasn't the time.

"Why are you being quiet?" Daniel asked as they began their trip in earnest.

"I don't want to disturb the driver."

Emily could see Daniel grin, but he didn't turn toward her, and she was grateful that he took his driving seriously.

"As soon as we get there, I'll run in the house and get Chloe right out," Emily promised. "We shouldn't stay out here longer than we need to."

"Thanks."

"I'll have to get her stuff too." Emily folded her hands on her lap. "I'll shut up now."

She saw Daniel's grin broaden, but she did, indeed, stay quiet the rest of the ride.

The usual 10-minute ride took nearly 30 minutes, and that was fine as far as Emily was concerned. Daniel had steered the SUV expertly up and down the winding back lanes, never bringing them anywhere near slipping off the road.

"Do you need to check on your cat?" Daniel asked when he stopped in the driveway at the Jenners' house.

"No." Emily's fingers had already gripped the handle of the car door. "Big Boy is very independent, and I have neighbors checking on him."

"OK, I'll keep the car running while you go in. I want to keep the heat on."

"Sounds good to me," Emily called as she exited the passenger side. Then she added before closing the door, "I hate to be cold."

She ran to the front door of the Jenner house—as best she could in the growing snow piles on the walk—and opened it with her key, which she kept on the same chain as her own car and house keys. Chloe came bounding toward her from the kitchen and placed her front paws on Emily's chest, something the well-behaved dog rarely did. Chloe must have grown concerned during the long day with no visitors.

"I'm here, sweetie," Emily said calmly as she gently slid Chloe's paws from her chest to the floor. The house was nearly pitch black, with only the headlights from the SUV illuminating the living room, which prompted Emily to reach to switch on a table lamp. It clicked, but no light turned on. She fumbled her way to where she remembered the other table lamp was, Chloe practically attached to her thighs, and nothing happened there either.

"Oh, dear." Emily patted the Lab's head. "You've lost electricity, haven't you?" The house wasn't cold, and Emily guessed that the power probably hadn't been out long. She switched on the mini flashlight on her keychain and made her way to the kitchen.

Chloe continued to stay close to Emily, and when they reached the kitchen, Emily grabbed three of the big dog treats and put them in Chloe's food bowl on the floor. The dog scarfed down all three immediately.

Although the food dish had been empty, the other bowl on the floor had water in it. Chloe's fancy water bowl was hooked up to the Jenners' water source, keeping the receptacle filled at all times. Again, Emily determined that the power must have only recently shut off if the bowl still held water.

She rubbed Chloe's fur. Satisfied for now, Chloe sat by her bowls while Emily shined her flashlight into the cabinets. She got out two plastic bags and filled them from the bags of dog food and treats, and she pulled out two new clean bowls and several chew toys.

Lastly, Emily grabbed the Lab's leash. Chloe jumped to her feet and frantically circled Emily several times. Emily clicked the leash on the big dog's collar, and Chloe yanked her human friend to the door. They stepped outside, and as Emily locked the door behind her, Chloe relieved herself on the front lawn. The dog wasn't thrilled with snowy hindquarters, though, and she shook herself vehemently, spewing snow all over Emily.

Daniel jumped from the car to help. "Chloe!" he chastised. The dog ran to Daniel and pushed her nose and then her midsection hard against his legs.

"Chloe is not the best guard dog," Emily explained, laughing. "Looks like she thinks you're her new best friend."

Daniel patted the dog's side as Chloe's tail pounded the back of his thighs. "Any friend of Emily's," Daniel said to Chloe, "is a friend of mine."

Chloe let out a quick bark of agreement.

"How do we get her into the SUV?" Daniel asked.

Emily smiled. "Fortunately, this dog loves to take drives. I'll show you." She opened the rear door behind the driver's seat and patted the bench. Chloe barked again, did a quick lick of Emily's hand on the seat, and jumped up. The dog bounded to the other window, looked out, turned around, sniffed the leather, and then plopped down. Emily could have sworn the Labrador Retriever was smiling.

Daniel must have thought the same thing because he shook his head and laughed. "OK, let's hit the road."

He started to walk with Emily to the other side of the car, but Emily put a hand on his chest. He had opened his coat at some point, and Emily could feel his strong muscles tense beneath her palm. "I know you're a gentleman," she said. "But the snow is getting deep, and it will take you too long to go around to open my door and then go back to get in your own side."

Daniel nodded and climbed in the driver's side while Emily trudged behind the Buick and put Chloe's things in the back. Then she walked around to the passenger side and lifted herself up and in. Before turning to settle in her seat, she kicked the snow off her boots and brushed what she could off her pants. The driveway wasn't icy, but the snow piles were growing.

As soon as Emily had her seatbelt on, Daniel eased the big vehicle out of the driveway and started slowly down the road. It seemed darker than before, and as they drove further away from Emily and the Jenners' neighborhood, the lights from the homes along the roads grew farther and farther apart. For a while, only a few dots of light blinked through the swirl of the snowstorm, like stars on a cloudy night. Until there were none.

"The visibility is terrible," Daniel muttered, almost to himself. Emily wondered if he even remembered she was with him in the car. He yanked off his hat in frustration and put it on the dashboard. "I can't even see the houses."

"There aren't any homes on this road," Emily admitted. She was hoping Daniel couldn't hear the slight tremble in her voice. "On the left is the far end of a working farm. And this," she continued, tapping the window on her side and gazing out, "is that park I was telling you about."

Daniel audibly gulped. "You mean the one where you can walk and walk for acres and not see a soul?"

Emily sighed. "Yes," she said quietly.

At that moment, Chloe sat up and began to whimper softly in the back seat. "I think she senses our concern," Emily said to Daniel and then twisted around to pat her friend. "It's OK, girl. Daniel is a great driver." Chloe quieted and licked Emily's hand.

Even though Daniel had already been driving only about 15 miles an hour, Emily could feel him slow the vehicle even more.

His lips were curled inward in concentration. "This is a great SUV, but I'm starting to feel the tires slip," he observed. "I have to continue the momentum to keep us from getting stuck, but I'm worried about staying on the road."

Even though he had just articulated his concern, as Daniel steered a 90-degree right turn at a barely moving speed, Emily was still shocked when the tires could not grip the asphalt, and all three of them drove headfirst over the side of the road.

# CHAPTER TWENTY-THREE

Without thinking, Daniel squeezed his eyes tightly as the SUV slammed into the ground and forced his body back against his seat and then forward again, gripped hard by the shoulder belt. When he stopped moving, he opened his eyes as quickly as possible—only to see the front windshield covered in white snow sprinkled with brown sticks and mud. He continued to stare forward for a few seconds and then heard Emily loudly gulp air.

"Emily, are you OK?"

She turned, and even in the dark, he could see her pale cheeks and forehead. She took in a shaky breath. "Yeah. You?"

"Yeah."

"I think I was holding my breath that whole time. What happened?"

"Uh ..."

"Wait," Emily corrected herself and began speaking rapidly. "I know what happened. We're in a ditch. It's just that it happened so fast. I always thought that when a crisis like this happened, it would all be in slow motion." She clamped her mouth shut. Then she said again, "It happened so fast."

"I know."

Both of their seatbelts had locked, but their chests were leaning forward against the locked strip of material. They both squirmed in their seats, trying to get their bearings.

Suddenly Emily yelled, "Chloe!" and she jerked to look behind her.

Chloe was in the rear of the Encore. The dog whimpered and cautiously moved downward to the back seat. Emily quickly unclipped her seatbelt and turned to wrap her arms around the big dog's neck and bury her face into fur. "You're OK!"

"She must have jumped to the back when our forward motion pushed us all backward," Daniel observed. He chuckled under his breath. "Smart dog."

He unclipped his own belt and winced as he suddenly realized that the lower-right side of his chest was throbbing painfully. He figured that the locking mechanism of the seat belt must have broken or, at the least, bruised a rib or two. Out of the corner of his eye, he saw Emily, still clutching Chloe, turn to him. "You're hurt!" she declared.

"I'm OK," Daniel assured her. "Just a bruise, I'm sure." He winced again.

"Oh, Daniel."

"It's fine." He gingerly twisted himself to look out the back window and assess where they were. He could see grey sky and breathed a sigh of relief; he had been a bit scared that they had been buried in a snowdrift. From where the sky seemed to meet the sides of the ditch, he guessed they were about 12 feet below the road. He pulled the lever to open his driver-side door. It opened about a foot and then met hard ground.

Daniel cursed under his breath.

Emily turned and reached for her own door. It opened much wider, but she immediately reclosed it as snow poured in from the top of the door.

Another expletive escaped from Daniel's lips.

"Sorry, Emmy," he said. "But this really stinks."

"I know," she replied. "And if there ever is a good time for a curse word, this is it!" She laughed, and then yelled "Ow!" and put her right hand to the side of her head.

Daniel felt his heart lurch. "What's wrong?"

"It's OK." Emily grimaced. "I must have banged my head against the side of the window." By her strained voice, Daniel could tell she was trying to make her tone light. She pulled her fingers away from her head and looked at them. "No worries. I'm not bleeding. I had just suddenly become aware of the fact that I have a pounding headache." She rubbed her head again.

Then Emily began to laugh. Daniel wasn't sure if she had a concussion and had lost some sense, but as she continued to laugh harder, he too began to chuckle. And then he was wincing and holding his injured side as he broke into a full guffaw.

Emily grabbed his hand, and the two laughed almost hysterically for about a minute. Finally, Chloe whimpered again and put her face between the two of them in the front seats, looking worriedly at one and then the other.

Reluctantly, Daniel pulled his hand from Emily's and ruffled the dog's fur. "It's OK, girl," he said. "We're just in shock. We'll calm down as soon as we start to get cold."

Emily shivered. "I'm already a little bit cold. Can you at least turn on the heat?"

Daniel turned the key, which was still in the ignition, and heard only a click. The car did not turn over.

"Uh-oh," Emily said. "That's not good."

Daniel turned to her and tried to grin. "I know. You must have told me 15 times on the slopes today that you hate to be cold."

He noticed that Emily was no longer smiling, and his face grew serious to match hers.

"No, really," Emily said forcefully. "I truly hate to be cold. I get a little panicky if I can't get warm. Can you turn on the accessories?"

Daniel took her hand again. "It'll be OK," he soothed. "But the heat won't work even with the ACC on. Hey, didn't you grab Chloe's blanket before you left the Jenners'? I'm sure I saw you put a blanket in the back. And if Chloe hasn't wet on it, it should still be dry."

Emily nodded but held onto Daniel's hand, even as he had turned slowly and carefully, intending to climb toward the back of the SUV.

"I'll get it," she said, lightly holding him in his seat. "I don't think you should be doing much twisting. First, let's see if we can get a signal to call for help. Cell service in this area isn't much good to begin with. I can't imagine it's better from a ditch!"

She unzipped her side coat pocket and pulled out her cell. The phone came right to life when she swiped the face. "It's still about 60% charged!" Daniel watched her face light up and then just as quickly go dark.

"I don't have any bars," Emily said quietly. She nodded decisively. "I'll try 911 anyway. Sometimes that works, right? Emergency service only or whatever?"

She tapped three numbers, put the phone to her ear, and waited.

Daniel pulled his own phone from his left front pocket. "I don't have anything either, and my phone is about to die anyway." He tapped his phone as well and put it on speaker phone, but nothing came out.

Each of them tried several more times with no luck. Finally, when Daniel saw that Emily's taps on her phone were becoming agitated jabs, he put his hand on her hands to still them. Then he said, "Hey, reach into the glove compartment and look for a phone."

"What?" She looked up at him, and his heart wrenched at the fear and confusion he saw on her pale face.

"Before we left, all of us put our work cell phones in the glove compartment." Daniel hoped his calm tone would quiet Emily's concerns. "It was a ceremonious 'unplugging' for the weekend. Our network provider for our work phones is better than the one I have for my home phone."

Emily popped the compartment and pulled something out. It was, indeed, a phone.

# CHAPTER TWENTY-FOUR

"That one's mine," Daniel said hopefully, as he took the cell from Emily and turned it on. His foot jiggled impatiently as he waited for it to gain full power.

"I think I have one bar!" he finally cried.

Emily puffed out a relieved-sounding breath as Daniel tried to make a call. He got nothing after three tries to 911, so he scrolled to his contacts and found Jon's number. He tapped that and put the phone to his ear.

"I'm getting something!"

From the other end of the line, besides a lot of static, Daniel heard, "Yo … are …? … hear …?"

"Jon, it's me, Daniel. Can you hear me? We've been in an accident."

"Dude? … hear …?"

"We're probably about 10 miles away," Daniel continued, hoping beyond hope that his friend could make out a few of his words.

"Dan? Where …?" The phone went silent—not even static anymore.

Daniel dialed again. This time, there was no ring. He tried several more times but could not connect again.

"Well," he said finally. "I guess we need a plan B."

"What are we going to do?" Emily's voice sounded an octave higher than usual. "I'm starting to get really cold."

Daniel quickly assessed his friend and saw that she was growing even paler than earlier. Her blue eyes looked huge in her white face. He had the fleeting thought that she looked like the porcelain doll that his grandmother kept in her curio—the one that always frightened him when he was little.

"I'm going to take this phone with me and start walking," Daniel said decisively. "You keep trying to call someone on your phone, and I'll work on mine."

"No!" Emily exclaimed, nearly shouting. She grabbed his arm with both hands, and he flinched in pain. She loosened her grip but still held on.

"Well, we can't stay here waiting until somebody finds us," Daniel said quietly. He gently pried her fingers from his arm. "No one is going out in this storm. And this ditch is deep; they won't see us from the road."

Emily looked down as she grabbed his hand. Then she gasped. "Our Fitbit watches! They have GPS. Someone can find us!"

Daniel's shook his head, and he knew his smile didn't meet his eyes. "That's true. But that kind of search may not happen for hours, maybe days. We need to act now. Listen, I'll walk back the way we came. There were a couple of houses on one of these back roads, I remember."

Emily made a noise that seemed like a small wail. "I'm sorry. I have no sense of direction. I know these roads when I'm driving them, but I'm not exactly sure where we are. I don't know where the closest houses are."

"It's OK," Daniel assured her. "I know I saw lights not too long ago, and we weren't driving very fast. It shouldn't be too far away."

"But what if it is?"

"How about this?" Daniel began. "I'll walk for an hour. If I haven't gotten cell service or seen a house, I'll come back."

"What should I do in the meantime?"

"Well, first get that blanket. Maybe snuggle under it with Chloe in the back seat. Keep trying your phone."

"Maybe we should all go together," Emily suggested. She nodded frantically, obviously trying to convince herself. "You're pretty hurt, and I hate being the helpless female back in the car."

That made Daniel laugh out loud. "You are *not* a helpless female," he said, "although that 'I hate to be cold' stuff does sound a bit wimpy."

Emily made a slapping motion near Daniel's face. "Stop," she said, but she was finally smiling again, just a bit. "I get really cranky when I'm cold."

"The thing is," Daniel said soberly, "if we split up, we have a better chance of being found. I know where the car is, and you know where I'm heading. I won't deviate from the way we came."

Emily sighed and sat up straighter. She folded her arms in front of herself. "You're right. I'll hold down the fort. Leave the keys. I'll keep trying the car. If it starts, maybe we can get both heat and Bluetooth."

Emily began rummaging on the floor. She picked up her keychain and began fumbling with it. "I'm giving you my little flashlight," she explained, continuing to work at the metal loop. "Ta da!" She lifted it up and handed it to Daniel.

"Thanks." Daniel flicked the mini light on and off and then pocketed it.

The two sat there for a few minutes, and Daniel figured that neither wanted to begin taking the next steps of plan B. Only the sound of their breathing whistled lightly in the air. Even Chloe's breaths were soft and steady.

"Uh, I'm going to have to crawl over you to get out," Daniel finally said, shrugging apologetically.

"No, you'll hurt your chest if I'm in the way. I've got to climb out anyway to get the blanket, so I'll go first. But wait a sec." Emily took a deep breath and continued, "I hope this doesn't bother you, but can I pray with you first? It would really help me avoid that cranky stage."

"Sure." Daniel agreed more quickly than he would have expected. "You know that I'm at that point in life where I don't think prayer can help, but right now, as far as I'm concerned, it can't hurt. They say there are no atheists in foxholes."

"And ditches, apparently," Emily agreed. She took one of Daniel's gloved hands in hers. He brought his other hand around his side and took her free palm. She glanced at their joined hands, looked up at Daniel, and seemed to beam at him. Chloe rested her long nose on Emily's shoulder.

"OK," Emily began. "God, we're really scared. At least I am." Chloe whined in agreement, which lightened things up a bit, and Emily snickered. "Please keep us safe and bring help soon. Keep Daniel safe on his walk, and keep me safe—and warm—in the car. In Jesus' name, we ask you. Amen."

"That was quick," Daniel observed. He had opened his eyes to look at her but kept her hands in his.

"Hey, God knows what we need," Emily pointed out. "I guess I should have also apologized to Him in advance for my crankiness."

Daniel shook his head. "You are something else." Then he got serious. "Here's what we need to do: You lean toward me and then open your door and let as much snow as possible fall to the ground —hopefully *outside* the car. Then jump out and run around to the back to get the blanket and anything else warm that might be back there. I'll follow you out and try to climb up this stupid embankment."

Emily followed Daniel's instructions. As she leaned into him— gently so as to avoid putting pressure against his bruised chest, he realized that her closeness calmed him. Despite the many layers of clothes between them, he felt a sense of her inner calm, and that warmed his whole being. And besides that, he just liked being that close to her. Even in a puffy jacket and thick pants, and all scrunched up against him, she looked adorable. For a moment, he was tempted to tell her again how he felt about her, but as she shifted, and he grimaced at the pressure and pain, he realized that that would have to wait.

Far from the door now, Emily stretched her foot, put the toe of her boot under the handle of the door, and pulled the metal arm toward her. The door unlatched, and she kicked it out and snatched her leg back toward herself to avoid the falling snow piles.

Because of her quick movements, the snow that had built up on top of the SUV and around them came crashing down almost immediately. Inside, it echoed like a true avalanche, nearly blocking out the screech of Emily's yell and Daniel's curse.

When the noise stopped, the silence was so abrupt and so total that the two stayed where they were for a good minute. Daniel could hear his own heart beating even through his down coat. He took a deep breath in and realized that he must have been holding his breath. The effort stabbed his ribs, though, and he winced.

Emily jerked away from him and toward the open door. "Sorry," she said.

"Me, too," Daniel replied. "I didn't mean to curse again. I usually don't do that very much."

"No worries," Emily said. "But let's move it before I get cold feet. Literally!"

# CHAPTER TWENTY-FIVE

E mily lunged out the door and felt her feet drown in the snow. Even with her long legs, the snow drift gurgled up past her boots and tried to reach her knees.

"Rats!" she exclaimed.

When she looked back toward the inside of the SUV, she watched Daniel carefully lean toward where she was standing and then actually laugh. "I guess that's your expletive for the day," he said. "It must be bad."

"Shush!" she admonished. "It's nasty. Trust me: I'm not 'running' to the back of the car. It's more like swimming!"

Emily began to forge her way to the SUV's rear, hugging the automobile as she moved.

"Take your time," Daniel advised. "I have to find my baseball cap anyway."

"I saw it on the floor," Emily called back.

A few seconds later, she saw Daniel's head appear out of the passenger side door. He had flicked on her flashlight and was pointing it toward the side of the Encore so she could see better. He swung his feet around and stomped to the ground. The snow came high on his shins, but Emily figured he still had better maneuverability than she did.

Still, she got to the back more quickly than she expected. After lifting the hatch, she pulled out the dog's blanket, a big, well-worn, once-colorful cotton quilt. Then she immediately reshut the hatch. In the meantime, Chloe had shimmied herself to the front passenger seat and was poking her nose out anxiously into the cold air. For some reason, seeing Chloe hanging out of the car door with her head by Daniel's side warmed Emily's heart.

Daniel turned toward the dog and lifted his arms in an "I can't believe it" gesture. "Back in the car, Chloe" he commanded. Chloe immediately shrunk back in and returned to the back seat. She pressed her face against the back window to watch the human make his way along the side of the Encore.

Daniel reached Emily behind the SUV and took her elbows. "Stay here and stay warm." He used the same voice he had just used with Chloe, which made Emily smile to herself.

"You stay warm, too." Emily used the same commanding tone. Then she softened. "And don't try to be heroic. Just do what you need to do. And remember: One hour out, and if nothing, come back."

Daniel nodded, and the snow that had already accumulated on the brim of his hat fell from his head. Pulling out his phone, he said, "Look. It's exactly 9:30." Then he frowned. "Wow. It's later than I thought. Anyway, I'll walk until 10:30 and turn right around if I don't see anyone."

Emily gasped. "You won't be back here until 11:30, nearly midnight," she observed in a near-whisper. "Gosh."

The two stood quietly for a moment.

"Let's go," Emily suddenly announced, lifting her head. Instinctively, she pulled on Daniel's arms, bringing his lips close to hers. She kissed him briefly but warmly. "Be careful."

Daniel's grin was wide when he pulled back to look at her, and even in the cold, she could feel her cheeks warm. "Thank you," he said.

Emily knew that those two words were meant to cover so very many things.

The wind had been blowing from the direction of the street. That meant that the snow on the side of the embankment closest to the road was not as deep as it was in the gully. After Daniel moved past Emily, she watched as he was able to get a few solid footholds and thus scramble as quickly as he could to the top of the ditch. When he got to the top, he clutched his side and seemed to be gasping for air. But before she could decide to go see if he was OK, he was standing on the road and brushing the snow off his clothes.

Emily hesitated and then threw herself into the passenger side and shut the door. He waved, and she reached across to honk the horn, which actually still worked. She licked her lips, still tasting their gentle kiss, and them clambering to the back seat to join Chloe.

When she looked out the window again, Daniel was gone.

Emily settled carefully in the back seat next to Chloe. Then she reached her arms up and wrapped them around the neck of the trembling dog.

"It's OK, girl. We're together. We'll be all right. As long as we can stay warm, we'll be fine." She pulled the blanket around the two of them. It smelled of sweaty dog, but it was soft and mostly dry, and she snuggled into it.

Chloe began to calm down at the tone of the soothing voice. The Lab nuzzled Emily's neck and then rested her snout on Emily's shoulder.

They sat there huddled together for several minutes. Then Emily moved aside to pull her phone out of her pocket. Chloe took that moment to leap to the rear of the SUV.

Emily smiled at that and tried 911 again. "You do not like to sit still, do you?"

When the connection didn't go through, Emily shut her phone and looked at the dog. Chloe was pacing in circles in the small back hatch area and pawing at the floor.

"Uh-oh. You need to go out, don't you?"

The dog lifted her head, a desperate look in her brown eyes.

"OK, OK. I'm taking you out. We don't want you using this car as your bathroom. We'll die of the fumes!"

She quickly tumbled to the front of the SUV again, but her quick movements caused her head to pound once more. She sat for a few moments, holding her head with both hands, but at Chloe's renewed whimpering, she opened the passenger door. This time, thankfully, she was not pelted with built-up snow, only with the falling precipitation still coming down from the storm. Without the flashlight, it was darker than before, so she hugged the side of the SUV as she had earlier, and she followed, as best she could, the path she had originally made to the back of the car. She lifted the hatch, and Chloe flew out.

Emily turned on her phone to provide light that allowed them both to see. The dog immediately squatted and did her business. When Chloe was done, she stood and looked down at the snow, which reached nearly to the top of her spindly legs. She tried to shake herself but couldn't. So she leaped into the back of the car and shook herself inside the SUV.

"Chloe!" Emily exclaimed. "Come on. We need to keep it dry in there."

Chloe let out a single happy bark and sat.

Emily released an exasperated sigh. She put her phone back in her coat pocket, closed the hatch, and spider-walked the SUV again to get to the door. Then she sat herself in the passenger seat, grabbed the blanket from the back, and wrapped it close around her.

She yanked out her phone once more, hoping to call Suzie, and still couldn't get a signal. She tried 911 again, but nothing happened. She sat for a few long minutes and then tried again.

It was hauntingly dark and silent, and the dog-fur smell was becoming less comforting and more rank. She knew she should probably save the battery on her phone, but turning it on every few minutes to try to call someone made her feel less alone—and less helpless. On the other hand, seeing the clock every minute she turned her cell display on was depressing her. Time was moving very slowly.

After about a half-hour, Emily heard the soft but steady snore of her companion. She turned around in the seat and could just barely see a bump that was the top of Chloe's haunches. The dog had hunkered down in the back section of the SUV and fallen asleep.

Emily smiled to herself and said faintly, "At least one of us isn't scared."

*I'm not really scared per se,* Emily told God silently. *I know someone will get us eventually. I'm more, I guess, worried. I'm not really sure what to do, and I don't think I can handle being too cold. I'm OK now, but it's getting colder.*

As she prayed, she could feel tears begin to form. She shook her head. "I'm not going to cry," she said aloud. At the sound, Chloe poked her head up and climbed to the rear seat to get closer to Emily. The dog butted her big head under Emily's arm.

Emily took a fortifying breath. "We'll be fine," she told the dog.

# CHAPTER TWENTY-SIX

Although the snow was coming down fairly hard, the weird combination of blinding-white snow and pitch-black road gave Daniel a little reflective-like visibility as he trudged back toward the way he had driven earlier. He was able to make out the white line marking the right side of the curb, so he kept Emily's tiny flashlight off most of the time. About every 50 yards, he turned it on to get his bearings and to shine it ahead in the hopes of seeing signs of life—human signs, not wild ones. After a while, he realized that even the wild ones must be hiding in this weather. It was eerily quiet. In fact, the only sounds were the crunch of his footsteps and the rustling of tree branches—plus the deep, sharp breaths he took in from the icy air.

"God, please keep Emily safe," Daniel whispered on one of those expulsions of breath. "I'm OK, but you know she gets cold easily, and I'm worried that she'll start feeling distressed. Plus, keep me on track. Let me find help in the next hour. I don't want to go back to her empty-handed. Please."

Daniel stopped suddenly. He had been walking at as brisk a pace as the conditions allowed him, but he was shocked to realize that he had started praying while he walked. He actually laughed out loud.

"OK, God," he said, louder this time, looking up into the sky. The whirling snow made it look like the inside of a milkshake, he noticed tangentially. "Anyway, I guess I'm going to have to trust you on this one. We'll have it out about my brother's cult issue later, you and I, but for now, I just have to believe that you have all this in hand."

Daniel slogged on, not really thinking about much else except trying to find a building with a light on. Even a building without a light on would be welcome relief. He usually had a good sense of time and distance, but the sameness of the road and swirling flakes made it difficult to grasp any kind of physical or even mental landmarks. He knew he could usually walk fairly quickly, but the wind was impeding his progress, which meant he really didn't have a clue how far he was going. Early in his trek, he had stopped checking his Fitbit watch every 3 minutes when he had been convinced that those intervals had been more like 15 minutes. He figured now that it was time to check again. He didn't want to return to Emily without help, but he also didn't want to leave her for more than the two hours he had promised.

Daniel turned on the little flashlight and first shined the light in front of him, expecting to find, as all the other times before, nothing but illuminated slashes of snow. To his surprise and relief, the farthest wash of the flashlight faintly highlighted some sort of structure up ahead where the road bent. He pointed the light directly at the structure, and it looked to be a kind of storage building.

"Where there's a big shed, there's a human," Daniel declared, trying to convince himself. He picked up his pace, continuing to shine the light on the outline of the building.

As he neared the edifice, he realized with disappointment that it was much smaller than he had thought. It looked like a detached one-car garage. The wooden structure—he couldn't tell what color it was, but he could see the peeling paint—sat off the road by about 30 yards. And the way the snow was flattened in a straight line from the road to the building about 20 feet wide, with drifts on either side, Daniel figured that there was probably a small road or pathway that led to the garage.

Of course, that pathway was now covered fairly deeply with snow.

Daniel grimaced when he stepped off the clearer road into about a foot of the white stuff.

*There's got to be a house that owns this garage,* he thought. *There just has to be.*

He had kept his flashlight on since he first saw the structure, but the glow was beginning to fade. Desperately, he flicked the light in all directions, but except for the garage, he could see nothing but trees and snow. He clicked off the gadget and continued his slow march, keeping his eye on the ground to make sure he didn't leave the path.

Winded from moving as quickly as he could through the thick snow, and from the ever-present pain in his ribs, Daniel finally reached the garage. One of the large, barn-like doors was not closed and was swinging in the wind. He let himself into the refuge of the building and pulled the door shut behind him, latching the long wooden arm from the one door into the groove of the door's twin.

He flashed the light quickly around his surroundings. He saw a wooden bench to the right of the door he had just entered, so he sat down and turned off his light to save the battery. Although the space he had briefly seen wasn't big, it was open. It had probably once served as a storage shed for yard equipment or tools, but it was empty now. Despite the slashes of holes made by rotting wood in the roof and walls, the space was relatively dry and most definitely felt warmer than outside.

Daniel realized he was still breathing heavily; the hike to this point had been more strenuous than he had anticipated. Now what? He longed to poke his head out the door to look around again, but he knew it was futile. There really weren't any houses or people nearby; he had clearly seen that earlier. He hadn't actually checked his watch earlier when he had seen the shed, but he felt sure he was nearing his hour time limit. He figured he could walk maybe another ten minutes, but he had failed.

Taking steady, but resigned, breaths, he pulled off his gloves and sat them on the bench beside him. He pulled out his phone and tapped it on. The display read 10:20. He was right—10 more minutes to turnaround time.

Instinctively, as he had been doing all night, he pressed redial and waited for the nothingness.

"Dan?"

Daniel quickly pulled his phone to his ear. "Jon, can you hear me?"

"It's about time," Jon replied. "Where the heck are you, man? I'm driving with a cop on a creepy back road in the middle of nowhere. Hey, do you know that police in the Poconos have really cool four-wheel drives? I'm not even sure what I'm driving in, but it's a fine ride!"

Daniel laughed with relief, and then grabbed his side at the stabbing pain.

"Dan, you there?"

After quickly catching his breath, Daniel spoke: "This is great! OK, the last street sign I saw was Creamery Lane. That was a cross street, and I'm maybe a quarter mile past that toward where Emily lives. Shoot! I'm not sure the name of the road I'm on."

He heard a muffled voice, and then immediately following that, he heard sirens over the phone.

"Dang!" Jon explained. "This guy knows where you are. You're on 532 or 552 or some backwoods route number like that. Oh, sorry, Officer."

"I'm in a shed off the road. I came in here for a little shelter. I'll walk back to the street."

"Wait," Jon said, and then he was obviously listening to another person speaking in the car. "Officer Sisko says he knows exactly where you are. That means you can stay in that garage and we'll find you. Hey, is Emily OK?"

"She's still in the ditch in the SUV with the dog. I wanted her to stay warm." Now, Daniel could hear the sirens in the air, no longer just through his phone, approaching from the direction of Emily's home. He was tempted to step outside to wave them down, but he didn't want to move for fear of losing the connection.

"Oh, man," Jon groaned. "We must have driven right past her on the way over. The visibility stinks."

The sirens grew closer, and Daniel finally began breathing more regularly. "I know exactly where she is," he started to explain.

Just then, he saw blue and red lights flash against the garage wall and heard the grind of wheels struggling through the snow. "I see you!" he exclaimed, and he stood up slowly, so as not to aggravate his injury. He leaned his head out the shed door. And just as he had expected, he lost phone service.

A very large, very bundled-up police officer stepped out of the driver's side of the police vehicle. Despite his bulky coat, he had no hat, and his shaved dark head was illuminated by the flashing lights of the car. He looked a little like a superhero. Behind him, the rear door flew open, and Jon stepped out. He trudged through the snow to his friend, and Daniel embraced him with a left-sided hug to avoid pressure on his chest.

"It's a Ford, go figure!" Jon said, as he pulled away and looked Daniel up and down. "What's wrong with your side?"

Before Daniel could answer, from the driver's side of the cruiser, Officer Sisko called out in a resonating bass voice. "Sir, if you are OK to move, let's go now. The snow isn't getting any less deep."

Jon, who was shorter than Daniel, put his arm around his friend's waist to walk him back to the car. Daniel winced, but he didn't think Jon heard him. "Hey, you're shivering, bud," Jon noticed.

"Well, I'm soaked, *bud*," Daniel said, emphasizing the term of endearment and trying to shrug it off. "We're in a snowstorm, you know."

"Testy, too," Jon teased.

"Grab that blanket from the back seat for him," the officer called from the car. "He's in shock."

Daniel started to protest, but for the first time since he had started walking again, he found himself gasping for breath, and he really was shivering. He gingerly sat down in the back seat. Jon wrapped the blanket around Daniel and moved up front to sit in the passenger seat, giving Daniel room to carefully stretch out in the back. As soon as they were settled in, the policeman pulled the cruiser back onto the street and headed toward Emily.

"Go slowly," Daniel advised. "I'm not exactly sure how far I walked, and we don't want to miss her again."

"We won't," Officer Sisko assured them. "I've got skills." He flipped a switch on his console, and a bright white searchlight shined from the roof of the cruiser to the left side of the road.

"Cool," Daniel and Jon both said together.

# CHAPTER TWENTY-SEVEN

"OK, Chloe, I'm so cold that it hurts," Emily declared. The dog picked up on the woman's rising fear and leaned forward in the car to lick Emily's cheek.

Emily shivered and wrapped her arms around Chloe's neck, pulling the blanket around both of them once again. "It's been more than an hour. I'm sure he'll be back soon, but it's not as if he's bringing a heater with him! Even bundled up like this, my skin feels raw. It's like all of me is one big skinned knee."

Chloe nuzzled further into her friend's side as Emily continued to speak.

"I'm babbling to a dog, and I don't care. And seeing my breath in the air is freaking me out. You know what. I bet it's just as cold outside as it is in here. Maybe it's even warmer outside. They say snow is like a blanket, right? Let's go out and see."

On the word "outside," Chloe had begun thumping her tail, and she lifted her front paws in a little excited jump.

"You've got fur, no fair." Emily laughed and then clicked the leash back on the big yellow dog's collar. "OK. Let's give it a try."

Opening the passenger door was way more difficult than earlier, as the snow was continuing to fall and build up outside in the ditch.

Emily pushed her right shoulder against the door to help with leverage. Her head still hurt, but it wasn't throbbing any longer, and she figured she probably didn't have a concussion. Thus, aside from being cold, she still had a bit of energy. She squeezed out of the car, closed the door, and pulled hard on the rear door to let the dog out. Chloe leaped into the snow. And while Emily closed the back door with both hands, Chloe quickly dashed up the side of the gully and into the woods.

～

D aniel sat in silence as Officer Sisko steered his way around the winding, dark, slick roads. The policeman was taking his time, and Daniel bit his tongue to keep from shouting for him to drive faster. Daniel knew this was the right way to manage travel in the storm, but it seemed to be taking so long!

Finally, as they rounded yet another curve, the roof light of the police car illuminated Jerry's SUV in the ditch.

"There she is!" Daniel shouted, but Officer Sisko was already slowing to a stop on the shoulder of the road.

"Wait," the policeman commanded. "Don't get out yet. First, are you sure she wasn't injured?"

"Yes," Daniel responded sharply, frustrated with not being able to run to Emily's aid. "She's in the front seat. The dog's in the back."

"You stay here," Officer Sisko said, again with that deep, firm voice. "You don't look very good, and I don't feel like having to carry two of you up that embankment."

Daniel knew he didn't have the stamina to protest, and he also knew he would have lost the argument anyway. When the officer opened the door to get out and the cruiser's inside light went on, Daniel glanced at himself in the rearview mirror. Even in the dim light, he could tell he was pale.

The large policeman was surprisingly nimble. He managed to slip down the side of the ditch and move quickly around to the passenger side of the stranded SUV. Under the bright police searchlight, Daniel and Jon could see him open the passenger-side door. Then the officer leaned half his body into the SUV. Finally, he pulled himself back out and closed the door.

Sitting in the rear of the police vehicle, Daniel couldn't open his door. "Jon, ask him what the heck the problem is."

Jon stepped out of the car. "What's up?" he yelled to the officer down in the gully. The wind had picked up again, and Daniel figured Jon knew he had to shout for his voice to carry.

"Nobody here."

"Let me out, let me out, Jon." Daniel futilely pawed at the back door.

Jon opened the door for his friend, and despite his pain and cold, Daniel propelled himself out and then skidded on his rump in the snow down the ditch, yelling in pain as he slid. At the bottom, he clutched at his side and caught his breath. Then he stood up slowly and carefully climbed around to the side of the car.

In the bright searchlight, he caught Officer Sisko's glance and his raised eyebrow. "She's not there."

Daniel yanked open the side back door and then looked at the officer. "Where would she go?" Daniel finally asked desperately, with his hand still on the open door.

"I was going to ask you that."

Daniel turned and faced the woods. "Emily!" He waited and then shouted again: "Emmy! Where are you?" He leaned forward to scramble up the ditch on the woods side, but the effort had finally gotten to him, and he slumped against the SUV.

Jon had cautiously followed Daniel into the gully, and now he placed his hand on his friend's shoulder. "Hey, maybe we should call the dog's name, just in case Emily can't respond or anything."

Daniel gasped. "What?"

"I'm sure she's fine," Jon said quickly. "But, hey, dogs are supposed to have better hearing than humans anyway, right?"

Daniel let his friend put his arm gently around Daniel's waist and begin to help him up the other side of the ditch.

"Chloe!" Daniel yelled.

"Chloe!" Jon echoed when they reached the edge of the trees.

As Daniel and Jon continued to call out for Emily and Chloe, Officer Sisko slowly climbed back up the other side of the embankment to the squad car. He flipped on the siren once and then flipped it off. Then he stepped back out of the car.

"She probably can't hear you calling," he shouted across the ditch to the men on the other side. "The wind is sucking up all our sound, and your voices aren't carrying. I figure my good old siren should have pierced this wind. If she's close, she'll hear that." He flipped the siren on and off again.

"But we won't hear her!" Daniel started for the woods.

"You can't just start walking." Jon squeezed Daniel a little tighter, and Daniel cried out in pain loudly this time. "Whoa, you're really hurt; you shouldn't be doing this." Jon turned his friend to face him and waited until Daniel glared at him. "Emily could be anywhere. I think we need to be the ones to wait for her to find her way back to us."

# CHAPTER TWENTY-EIGHT

Chloe's ears went up the exact moment that Emily heard the police siren. The dog immediately started barking her heart out, but Emily realized that even that sharp sound was not cutting through the loud screeching of the wind. Emily patted the side of Chloe's neck. "Quiet down, sweet girl. They can't hear you."

Earlier, after Chloe had dashed off, Emily had finally caught up with her in the woods and bent down to grab the dog's leash. But when she did, the top of Emily's pants had gotten caught on a low-hanging tree limb. She couldn't untangle herself, and the branch was too big and heavy to break off. In addition, the corduroy of her jeans was too thick and now too wet for her to rip it away from the tree. At one point, she had considered the option of removing her pants all together, but she had to be about 50 yards from the SUV, and she knew she would have gotten frostbite before reaching the car. She thought about it again, now that she knew someone was nearby, but that still seemed a ridiculous idea.

Emily reached into her pocket and realized that she had left her phone in the car. "Seriously?" she said out loud. She tried to rustle tree branches to make noise, but even she couldn't hear that sound. She looked up. "OK, God. I know I'm not going to die or anything, but can we figure this out soon before I have to lose a toe or a finger?" She whimpered and brought her gloved hand up to tap her chin and think. *Sorry for being snarky,* she prayed, *but my feet and hands really hurt.*

The siren blasted again.

Chloe began whining. The dog looked at Emily and then looked in the direction that they had heard the siren, which Emily figured had to be right near where they had slid into the ditch. Chloe repeated the back-and-forth head movement and then gave a little bark of frustration. Emily pet the dog's head. Then she gasped and looked up again.

*Duh. I get it. It's a Lassie thing.*

She quickly unhooked Chloe's leash and pointed to the direction they had originally come. "Go get help, Lassie!"

Chloe tilted her head at Emily, who chuckled at the dog's confusion and rolled her eyes. "Go ahead, Chloe" she commanded. "Go find Daniel."

I n the end, it was a policeman and Jon whom Chloe led back to Emily and the offending branch. Jon moved behind Emily and, because he was at a more practical angle, was able to fairly quickly dislodge her caught corduroys from the tree.

Once free, Emily threw her arms around Jon's neck and held on. She buried her head into his shoulder and felt the tears immediately spill down her cheeks.

"Thank you, thank you," she breathed.

Chloe circled the three of them and barked excitedly, clearly both proud of her rescue and pleased that Emily was happy.

As Emily pulled back from Jon, she suddenly gasped. "Daniel! He went to look for help and he's hurt and—"

The officer cut her off. "He's back in the squad car, Miss" His voice was so deep and sonorous that Emily had no trouble hearing him over the wind. "Thick-headed mule. I practically had to handcuff him to keep him from coming with us."

"Oh, thank goodness," Emily exclaimed, finally truly smiling for the first time in hours. Then she added, "But why did you have to keep him from going with you?"

"He's pretty hurt—I'm guessing a few broken ribs," the policeman said. "You probably are, too. You're freezing and most likely in shock. Can you walk?"

Emily nodded. "Yes. I'm fine. Just really cold." As if on cue, her teeth began to chatter.

"I'm Officer Sisko," the policeman said calmly, stepping toward her. "And I'm going to pick you up and carry you until we get to the edge of the ditch, OK?"

"No, I'm—"

Emily squealed as the huge man easily lifted her off her feet. "I only asked if it was OK in order to be polite," he grumbled.

Officer Sisko's body warmth immediately flowed into Emily as if she were taking a hot bath. She put her arms around his neck and clung tightly. "Hey, where's your hat?" she asked suddenly.

He sighed and began walking out of the woods. "Didn't want to get it wet."

When they reached the top of the embankment, the policeman put Emily down. "OK, the best way for us to tackle this ditch is—"

As Emily nearly flew down one side of the gully and up the other, despite the thick snow, she thought she heard the officer say, "I guess she *isn't* hurt."

When she reached the squad car, Emily wrenched open the back door and then realized right away that she had startled Daniel awake. He turned to get out of the car, but she quickly slid in beside him, nudging him further in with her hip. She grabbed him by the elbows as he faced her.

"Oh, Daniel." Emily longed to hug him, but even though he was clearly relieved to see her, she could see the pain reflected on his face and his scrunched eyes. "You're getting worse. Just sit back."

By now, Officer Sisko and Jon had reached the cruiser. "We'll head to Urgent Care," the policeman explained. "There's one nearby, and one of the doctors lives next door to the clinic. He volunteered to walk over and man the fort during the storm, and I already called it in."

"Thank you, Officer Sisko," Emily said. "And thank you, God."

"That's right, Miss," the officer agreed. "'Thank you, God,' indeed."

Jon had led Chloe to the opposite side of the car and was nudging her into the back seat. "Do *not* sit on Daniel," Jon commanded, and then he moved around to sit again in the front passenger seat.

Officer Sisko maneuvered the car out of the back roads and onto a major highway; they reached Urgent Care in less than 10 minutes. During that time, everyone sat still and quiet, with only the whirr of the blasting heater and the soft chatter of Emily's teeth to fill the silence.

The Urgent Care building was the end structure in a small strip mall. Officer Sisko was able to pull along the side of the road. Although the parking lot was under more than a foot of snow, a kind soul had shoveled a rough path the short distance from the clinic door to the street.

The policeman and Jon jumped out of the car first, and a short, plump, white-haired man in light blue scrubs met them before they reached the door.

"Hey, doc, how should we bring these two in?" Officer Sisko asked. "Even with your walkway here, wheelchairs won't cut it. I guess I could carry the girl, but the guy's pretty big."

"I've got cardboard boxes to lay over the path," the doctor explained. "They're right by the door here, already cut up." He reached inside, and the two began laying the path.

As they did this, Jon opened the back door for Emily and then went around the other side of the car to open the door for Chloe and Daniel. Emily watched as Jon grabbed Chloe's leash.

When the doctor and officer wheeled two chairs onto the cardboard, both Emily and Daniel started to protest. But the evening had taken its toll on them, and their voices were weak. Officer Sisko quickly cut short their grumblings.

"Sit," he barked.

The two sat obediently.

"T-t-take him first." Emily had begun shivering again. "I think he b-b-broke his r-ribs."

The doctor smiled broadly, white teeth breaking into a round face already red from the short time outside in the cold. "That's sweet, ma'am. But you look like you might be in shock. Let's check you for frostbite."

There was a weak, high-pitched whine, and Emily was shocked to realize it had come from her own mouth. She looked over at Daniel, who had leaned his head against the back of the chair and closed his eyes but still had a face pinched in pain. And then she finally sobbed.

# CHAPTER TWENTY-NINE

For a rather rotund and out-of-shape-looking man, the doctor was quick and strong. In short order, he lifted Emily, laid her on an observation table, gently removed or cut off her wet clothes, and wrapped her with warm, dry blankets. She was embarrassed that she was crying like a lost child while he did all this, but his bedside manner was soothing and efficient. Emily realized she felt comfortable for the first time all night, although her fingers and toes were prickly. The doctor then placed her feet and hands in lukewarm water, and he explained that he was setting up an IV to help replace lost fluids.

Emily's sobbing finally slowed and then stopped, and she began taking fewer and fewer shuddering breaths. With surprising gentleness, the physician wiped her face with a soft tissue. And then the exhaustion hit her hard. "Am I OK?" Emily asked, less frightened now and more curious and sleepy.

"You're OK," the doctor replied, and even with her eyes closed, Emily could picture that red, round, smiling face. "We're just going to get more circulation back in those extremities." Then he added before Emily could ask as she dozed off, "And your friend and the dog will be fine, too."

Emily slid in and out of sleep, but when she finally fully awoke, her hands and feet had warm bandages on them, and she was down to only one blanket on top of her. She started to rise, and she realized that the doctor was standing right beside the table.

"Do you really feel OK to sit up?" he asked.

Slowly, Emily lifted herself to a sitting position and swung her legs over the table. She took a few deep breaths and then lowered herself gently to the floor, with the blanket still wrapped around her. She was glad to find that her toes no longer stung. They were sore, but she no longer felt as if they had pins in them.

She heard a knock on the door, and Daniel came in without waiting for a response. He walked cautiously and stiffly, but he was smiling, and he looked way more relaxed.

She smiled back at him. "How are you?" she asked.

"Oh, fine," Daniel replied, a little singsongy. "I just have a few minor hairline fractures, and Doc here gave me nice, strong painkillers. I have to ice my chest." He actually giggled. "Seems kind of silly after all the ice we've endured!"

Another knock came on the now-open door, and Jon walked in. "Are you guys ready yet?" he asked, pretending to complain. "You've been here, like, forever."

The doctor nodded and gave them all that big smile of his, indicating that the two patients could leave, but Emily blushed. "Um, I don't have clothes." She pointedly glanced down at her blanket attire.

"My wife brought over sweatpants and a sweatshirt," the doctor explained. "You'll swim in them, but we threw your pants away—sorry, but they weren't salvageable—and your other clothes are still too wet."

After Emily changed, and Daniel and Emily had thanked the doctor profusely, they followed Jon outside. It was very dark, but the snow had definitely subsided. Emily looked at her wrist for her watch, but it wasn't there. It was probably in the bag of stuff that the doctor had given Jon to take with them.

"I checked the clock inside," Daniel announced, still in that singsongy voice. "It's nearly 1:30 a.m."

Emily figured it had been about two hours since they arrived.

"I have your car, Emily," Jon explained, although he hadn't needed to say anything since it was the only car on the side of the road. "Sisko took me back to the hotel to get it, and Susie got your keys for me. She wanted to come, but I didn't want to risk having more of us out here than necessary."

"Thanks," Daniel said, and he clapped his left arm around his friend's shoulder.

Emily exchanged a look with Jon, and they shared a smile at Daniel's medicated behavior. Jon continued, "Besides, I think Jerry is very much enjoying comforting your worried friend, Suzie."

"And what about our man Ryan?" Daniel asked as they carefully bundled themselves into Emily's car, Daniel in the front passenger seat and Emily in the back.

"No idea." Jon shrugged as he slipped behind the wheel. "He hasn't been around the whole night. We haven't seen your friend, Brandon, either, Emily. For a while there, we saw Mr. Garrett just about every 15 minutes, though." He chuckled. "Every time the electricity goes out, the generator kicks on and then dies. He's getting quite the workout running down to the basement to tweak it!"

When they finally arrived back at the inn, Emily had barely enough strength to open the car door. Once the door was open, she stayed seated, catching her breath.

Through the white swirl of snow, there were only a few lights shining from the old stone and clapboard building.

"Like I said, the electricity has been on and off all night," Jon explained. "It looks like we're in a generator moment right now. Mr. Garrett seemed so frazzled that, a while ago, we started just staying out of his way."

The inn doors slid open, and Suzie sprinted into the parking lot, followed by Jerry.

Jon helped Emily the rest of the way out of the car. "We had all been hanging out in the lobby waiting to figure out what had happened to you guys," Jon explained. "Once Officer Sisko dropped me off after we took you both to the doc's, nobody wanted to go to sleep until you came back safely."

"Thank goodness you *are* back safely," Jerry said, and Emily could see a twinkle in his eye even in the dim night light. "There were only so many rounds of 'I Spy' that I could stomach!"

"Sorry about your car," Emily began.

"No worries," Jerry replied. "I was looking to upgrade to an Enclave this year anyway!"

Suzie launched herself at Emily, lifting her bedraggled friend off the ground in a hug. "Oh, my gosh," Suzie exclaimed. "We've been super worried. Even after Jon came back and said you guys were at Urgent Care and going to be OK, I really wanted to come be with you. I just kept praying."

After Suzie gently lowered Emily back to her feet, Emily grabbed her friend's hands and squeezed. "Thank you, thank you," Emily said. "It was major scary; I can't even begin to tell you. But we're back and we're fine."

Daniel popped out of his side of the car. "Great!" he agreed.

Emily laughed. "Well, Daniel broke a few ribs and is on painkillers, so he's 'greater' than I am, I think! I just want to go to sleep."

W hen Emily heard a loud click, she opened her eyes, blinked at the bright light in the room and glanced at the bedside clock: 11:09. She had slept more than 9 hours. Without picking up her head, she turned her face to the other side and saw Suzie struggling to kick the room door closed behind her as she balanced what looked like breakfast food and drink in both arms.

"Thank goodness that your chef got caught staying here because of the storm," Suzie said as she began carefully lowering plates and cups to the desktop. "A bunch of people left when they could, but Tom said he was scheduled to come back to cook for lunch anyway, so why not stay overnight and then serve breakfast? He seems really nice. He called the breakfast chef last night and told her to just stay home with her family."

Emily finally ventured to raise herself to a sitting position. She felt a little dizzy, but she was very aware of being warm and comfortable. She didn't remember dressing for bed the night before, but she realized she had on her favorite black-and-red-checked flannel pajamas and warm, fuzzy, black socks. She sighed contentedly.

Suzie rushed to her side and sat on the edge of the bed. "I'm not sure what that sound means. Are you sick or sore or cold or what?"

"It's an 'I'm really OK" sigh," Emily declared. "Suzie, it was crazy scary, and I was crazy cold. I knew we'd be found eventually, but I didn't think I'd be able to last very long. I was probably more wrecked emotionally than physically."

Suzie nodded and grabbed Emily's hand.

"Hey, where's Chloe?" Emily asked, swerving to get out of the other side of the bed.

Suzie held onto her friend's hand and tugged gently to keep Emily where she was. "She's in the boys' room," Suzie said. "I saw them earlier at breakfast, and they said Chole has been sleeping as soundly as you and Daniel."

"Is Daniel OK?"

"The last I heard," Suzie began as she rose and headed back to the desk, "he's still asleep."

"Good." Emily lifted her nose and sniffed the air. "Oh, my goodness. What is that incredible smell?"

Suzie giggled and turned her back to Emily, purposely hiding the plate she had picked back up off the desk. Then she swiveled with a flourish. "French toast with blueberries and, of course, powdered sugar!"

Emily scooched up on the bed, crossed her legs, and gratefully took the offered plate. She bent her head over the meal and breathed deeply. "Heaven!"

# CHAPTER THIRTY

After Emily had eaten everything Suzie had proffered—which, because Suzie was unsure what her friend would want, included the French toast plus bacon, scrambled eggs, and hash browns, not to mention orange juice and coffee—Emily finally got up to take a shower. Sometime during her meal, Jerry had called and asked Suzie to join the rest of the group in the room upstairs, so Suzie had left Emily to give her time and space to finish her breakfast and clean up.

The warm shower felt good, but Emily had definitely rested and eaten enough and was anxious to get back to her friends, which encouraged her not to linger long. Before heading upstairs, she went to the lobby, where Stacey was slumped awkwardly in the hard chair behind the front desk. Emily went to the girl and lightly shook her shoulder.

Stacey stirred and looked up at Emily with a confused and foggy stare.

Emily handed Stacey a room key and gently lifted the young woman to her feet. "Go crash in my room," Emily directed. "It's not as if anyone is checking in today." Both women looked out the glass lobby doors, which were covered in windblown snow.

Stacey smiled weakly at Emily and nodded her thanks. She tapped a few buttons on the front-desk phone and said to Emily, "I'm just transferring the incoming calls to the phone in your room, if that's OK."

"Sure."

Emily watched Stacey walk down the hall to the room where Emily and Suzie were staying. She waved as Stacey unlocked the door and entered. Then she headed to the elevators.

Because the inn was still running on the generator, there was printer paper on one of the elevators with a note that said to please take the stairs. Emily obeyed, walking the steps to the third floor and then knocking on room 324.

As soon as Jerry opened the door, Emily could hear the laughter spill into the hallway. When she entered, she chastised, "Hey, keep it down in here. You don't want the other guests to complain!"

"Seriously, Emily?" Jon asked. "There are no other guests!"

"That was a joke, Jon."

Daniel was sitting ultra-stiffly at the desk, finishing off his own breakfast. But he had looked up the minute Emily had arrived. She caught his eye and smiled. She could tell that the painkillers had begun to wear off as his face was a bit pale and pinched. But he managed a smile back. He looked vulnerable yet still sure and strong and delighted to see her.

"These guys are trying to make me laugh," he complained, "and it hurts."

Emily pouted in sympathy. "Well," she said, "you can tell them all the details about last night, and that will make them cry instead. It's like that scene in *Mary Poppins* where they have to get down from the ceiling of that 'I Love to Laugh' uncle guy, and the only way to stop laughing is to say they have to leave. Our way down is to talk about the crash."

Jerry scoffed. "And we're a captive audience. We actually *can't* leave. None of us is really sure where my SUV is anyway. My poor baby!"

As the rest of the group laughed, Daniel managed a small chuckle. He looked at Emily. He was glad he was more lucid now and could understand what was going on. Emily had way more color in her face than she had last night, and despite his own pain—he had taken only a half-dose of the pain killers earlier in the morning—he was thrilled at how healthy she looked.

Emily was looking around the room. "Hey, where's Ryan?"

Jon shook his head and shrugged. "We have no idea. Last night, he wasn't around much. He slept here and then disappeared early this morning. Where the heck could he be going?"

"No offense," Jerry said. "But your adventure in the ditch was our only entertainment."

Jon punched Jerry lightly in the arm, and Daniel recognized that he was very thankful for his friends.

Chloe had been curled under the desk at Daniel's feet, but she had stirred when she heard Emily's voice. Now the Labrador Retriever was pushing her nose against Daniel's knee, urging him to move aside.

Daniel twisted out of the way as carefully as he could to avoid getting jostled by the big dog. Chloe squeezed to freedom, leaped up, and slapped two big paws on Emily's shoulders.

"Fickle dog," Daniel grumbled. "I thought *I* was your best friend."

"Chloe didn't leave Daniel's bedside all night," Jon explained. "She slept, but she stirred every time that Daniel groaned."

"And he did that a lot," Jerry confirmed.

Emily gently pushed the dog off her chest but kept petting her. She caught Daniel's gaze and bit her bottom lip.

Daniel's spirits soared at the clearly worried look on Emily's face. Maybe he was wishing it, but he was sure he recognized that look from 20 years ago when Emily was a little girl at the beach. It was more than a friend's concern for another friend. She cared for him a lot.

"I'm really OK." Daniel cautiously stood and reached an arm out to her. "It hurts like crazy, but it will get better. And thank God you're

OK. I know you think that's just a platitude, but I mean it. Every time I woke up in pain last night, I thought, *Thank God Emily is OK.*"

Emily moved to him, the look on her face unreadable. She didn't hug him, as he was expecting her to do and what he braced for, but she did something even better. She cupped his cheeks in her hands and gently pulled his forehead to meet hers. "I'm so glad," she whispered. "And I'm glad, too, that if I had to have a traumatic experience like that, you were with me through it all."

She lightly pushed a fallen lock of hair off Daniel's forehead. Then she smiled as if she had an inside joke. Daniel scrunched his eyes quizzically, and Emily blushed. She leaned to his ear and murmured, "I have wanted to do that to your hair since I was five years old. It still feels like feathers."

Daniel wrapped an arm around her waist. Then he couldn't help himself: he kissed her. It was chaste and not very long, but he meant it to be soft and warm and sweet so that she knew how he felt. She was responsive and not surprised, and when he leaned back, she was smiling even brighter, and her cheeks were just a very light shade of pink.

"Ahem," Jon interrupted loudly.

Emily turned to the crowd in the room, and her face grew more red. Daniel's first thought was that she looked adorable when she was embarrassed. His second thought was that he was totally a goner when it came to her.

Everyone laughed, and Suzie turned to Jon and stage-whispered, "I guess she's not planning to fix me up with Daniel anymore." Emily just covered her face in her hands.

When the laughter in the room began to die down, Jerry announced, "OK, let's figure out what's going on outside of our little room."

"Good idea," Emily said, grateful to no longer be the center of attention. "I have to take Chloe out anyway. I'm sure no one thought to walk her."

"Actually, I took her out about an hour ago," Jon pointed out, his dark eyes sparkling and his chin lifted in mock defiance. "And I put water in a bowl, but I'm sure she's starved. Can we see what Tom might have in the restaurant for her?"

"Let's divide and conquer," Jerry said. He took command and assigned tasks. Daniel was to call the police station to discover what happened with the SUV. Suzie and Emily were tasked with finding food for Chloe.

"Jon and I will look for Ryan," Jerry confirmed. "It's pretty weird that he's been gone for hours. Like I said, there's not exactly much to do around here."

When the rest of the crew left the room to attend to their assignments, leaving Daniel at the desk to call the police station, Chloe whined and looked at Daniel with worry.

"It's OK, girl, she'll be right back," Daniel said and patted the dog. He took his breakfast plate, which had a few leftover pieces of toast and sausage, and put it down beside the water bowl that Jon had placed on the floor earlier. As Chloe dug in, Daniel picked up the phone.

# CHAPTER THIRTY-ONE

The women walked in comfortable silence down the stairs and into the restaurant. They found Tom seated at a table reading a paperback. When he looked up as they walked into the dining room, he cringed.

"I know, I know." He stood to meet them. "I still have to do the dishes. I figured no one else was coming for breakfast, and I could take a little break."

Emily lifted her hands, palms out, in a gesture of innocence. "No way would we criticize you!" Then she hugged him. "In fact, we can't thank you enough for feeding us in such style. You must be exhausted."

"Nah." Tom blushed. "I slept like a baby last night in one of the guest rooms—that is, of course, after I had heard you and your friend were OK."

"Thanks," Emily said, "We're actually here to try to find food for the dog."

Tom brightened. "I've got just the thing. I had basic baked chicken and pasta and was going to figure out what to do with it later on."

When Emily hesitated, Tom put a beefy arm around her. "I got three pups of my own," he assured her. "My wife has made me search online a million times for 'people foods dogs can eat.' These are fine."

After getting several plastic storage containers of "people foods dogs can eat," Emily and Suzie headed out of the restaurant. When they reached the bottom of the stairwell, Suzie turned, met Emily's eyes, and said, "Sooo," dragging out the o's.

Emily flushed. She had been doing a lot of that this morning. "So? So what?" She hoped she came across as clueless.

"Don't give me that," Suzie teased. "You are as red as, as red as …" Suzie looked around the empty hallway and then pointed back from where they came. "Well, as red as the tablecloths in the restaurant."

Both women laughed. "Sorry," Suzie admitted. "I could find a different red to compare you to if you really wanted me to. But don't change the subject. What's with you and Daniel? What happened in the SUV?"

"Nothing happened like you mean. But it was definitely a freaky time and then a transformational time. I really felt as if Daniel was—I don't know—*there* for me. And I was there for him." Emily paused. "It seems corny, I'm sure. But although I was super scared and definitely freezing, I felt as if everything was going to be all right. Of course, I knew that God was with us, giving us wisdom. But it felt as if Daniel knew God was there too. Suzie, Daniel even prayed with me!"

Her friend pulled Emily in for a hug. "I've been praying for you two." Suzie said. "It just seems right. You are good for each other."

"Thanks."

"Emily!" Stacey called from the doorway of Emily and Suzie's room. "Mrs. Garrett is on the phone from Orlando and wants to talk to you."

Emily and Suzie shared a look of curiosity as they walked into the room. Emily took the phone from Stacey and nodded her thanks.

"Hey, Kim," Emily said into the phone.

"Are you OK?" came the worried voice on the other end of the line.

"I'm fine. But this has to be the worst storm I've ever seen since I've lived here!" Emily pulled the drapes aside and looked out the window. "The snow has stopped, but it's still deep and blowing. I don't know when the snowplows will get here."

"I know," Kim Garrett replied. "There are no planes going in or out of the Allentown airport." She paused. "OK, I know this sounds odd, but I'm concerned about Milt. I can't get him on his cell phone, and he's not answering the phone in the office. Can you look around?"

"Sure," Emily replied. "But I wouldn't worry. Cell service has been really spotty. We can't find one of the guys in our group either. And Brandon and his girlfriend haven't been seen much, so maybe they are all hanging out together somewhere. Brandon probably has Milt holed up in a room, yakking at him to sell the inn!"

"Thanks." The older woman's voice reflected relief. "I'm sure you're right."

After Emily hung up, she said to Stacey and Suzie, "I'm going to take this food up to Chloe, and then Stacey and I need to do an all-out search for Mr. Garrett. Kim is worried. I'm sure he's fine, but we have to find him and tell him to call his wife."

"I'll come with you," Suzie said. She looked down at the young girl who had plopped down on a bed. "Stacey really needs to sleep."

After Suzie and Emily left the room, they once again took the stairs. When they reached the third floor and exited the stairway, Emily nearly bumped right into Brandon.

"I was just talking about you!" Emily greeted him with a grin. "Have you seen Mr. Garrett? Mrs. Garrett has been trying to contact him."

"No. Why do you think I saw him?" Brandon asked defensively.

Emily's grin faded. "I ...I just thought—"

Brandon continued to stare at her, prompting Emily to clear her throat. "Well, no one has seen you in a while, and no one has seen him, so we thought you might be together."

That seemed to relax Brandon, and he even rolled his eyes. "I've been caged up with a crazy woman," he said matter-of-factly. "Karen hates it here, and we can't leave. All she does is watch TV. And with the electricity going off fairly regularly, she freaks out with that same regularity!"

"It's been on all morning," Suzie said quietly.

"Yeah, well, the Garretts are really gonna have to sell after this storm," Brandon said. "And whoever buys it will bulldoze this old thing."

"Brandon!" Emily exclaimed. "I love this building."

"You should think about moving to Philly with me," Brandon said firmly. "Between the things constantly breaking here in the inn and the things creeping you out at the Jenners' place, you belong someplace better, safer."

Emily tilted her head at Brandon, studying him. "What do you mean 'things creeping me out at the Jenners' place'? What creepy things?"

Brandon looked guiltily at the ground. "I tried to go see you last week." His remorseful voice was so soft that Emily could barely hear him. "You were letting Chloe out, and I was walking through the bushes from your apartment. I saw you get scared." Brandon's chin came up defiantly. "I decided not to show myself. I figured you needed to see how desolate it is out here. You should be with me in the city."

"That was mean," Suzie chastised him.

Emily placed her hand on her friend's arm, and Suzie took a step back, taking the cue. "Here, I'll take the food to Chloe." Suzie accepted the bags from Emily. "Sorry. I realize you can fight your own battles."

After Suzie had knocked on the room where the men were staying and was let in, Emily moved back into the stairwell, holding the door for Brandon to follow so that they could talk privately.

"That *was* mean," Emily said when the door had closed behind the two of them. "But Brandon, where people live and what they like and what holds value for them—that's all different. God gives us different skills and interests. You're made for a city hotel. And I can tell you're good at it."

"But …"

"And I'm meant for here."

Brandon hesitated and then nodded. "You're right. It's frightening to make changes, and I was certainly comfortable with you. I keep looking at our time together as a couple as safe and familiar." He smiled ruefully. "I guess I'm still working out God's will for my life. And whatever that will is, it really *is* in the city." He started to turn away and then glanced meaningfully over his shoulder. "But it's *not* Karen."

Emily laughed and put out her right hand to shake, but Brandon turned and took her hand in both of his. "Thanks," he said. "I guess I was missing you and not really thinking about what that all meant. If you're open to it, I'd still like to be your friend."

"I'd like that, too."

# CHAPTER THIRTY-TWO

As Brandon finished speaking, the lights in the stairway flickered and went dark. Only the exit sign above the door continued to glow. Emily could see that there was no light at the bottom of the door, which indicated the hallway must have gone black as well. Before either of them could reach for the panic bar to push open the door, a small white light flickered in the hall. They watched as it grew closer, not moving. Someone was walking toward them, swinging a flashlight.

The door opened, and Emily gasped. All they could see was the outline of a tall man holding a cell phone in front of him, with a flashlight app lighting Emily and Brandon but keeping the man in shadow. The figure didn't say anything, and the door closed behind him.

Brandon stepped in front of Emily in a protective stance.

"It's just me," came Daniel's voice. He brought his phone light to his chin to enable the other two to see his face. His brows were tight together in annoyance.

Emily stepped around Brandon and grabbed Daniel's free hand. "Thank goodness. You scared the stuffing out of us." She glanced at Brandon, who seemed to have puffed out his chest. "I mean, you scared the stuffing out of *me* at least. It's pitch black!"

"Yeah, Dude," Brandon said as he sidestepped Daniel to open the door. "Listen, I gotta check on Karen. And Emily, you're right, you do belong here. But you may want to talk the Garretts into upgrading the electric!"

After Brandon had gone, Daniel asked, "What was that about?" He held the door open for Emily as they watched the other man move down the hall, his own cell phone also now lit up.

"Nothing. Or rather, Brandon and I were just giving each other a bit of closure." She nodded. "It was good."

Even in the dim light of Daniel's flashlight, she could see that he was still concerned. She hated to admit it, but his jealousy made her heart leap a little.

"Really," she said. "We're good. Brandon is moving on. Come on, now. Shine your light on the steps, and we'll head to the basement. The door is at the far end of the ballroom downstairs."

Emily released Daniel's hand but moved her own hand up to grab his elbow. She also sidled closer to him, their shoulders, hips, and legs moving almost in unison as they walked down the stairs. She had tucked herself into him for safety, so they could both follow the light together, but it still felt good just to have him close.

"I expect we'll finally see Milt Garrett at the basement door," Emily suggested. "He's got to go back down there and fix the generator again."

As they stepped into the dark ballroom, Emily pointed toward the far right of the room. The wood-paneled floor was mostly empty, with metal chairs and matching round tables folded up against the walls. Light filtered in through closed blinds, but it was still overcast outside, and Daniel kept his flashlight on. They were walking toward the basement door when they both stopped midway in the ballroom.

"What's that against the door?" Daniel asked, voicing Emily's concern as well. "It looks like a 2-by-4 right in front of the door."

In truth, the ambient light in the room was bright enough for them to walk across the floor without falling. Daniel turned off the light on his phone and jogged ahead, with Emily not far behind. He knocked away the wooden board, which had been shoved up under the doorknob, effectively locking in anyone who was in the basement.

Daniel yanked open the door, and before they could call out, they heard, "Finally!"

"That's Mr. Garrett!" Emily exclaimed as she practically sprinted down the stairs, hands balancing herself on the railings on both sides but slipping every few steps on the worn, brown industrial carpet. The older man met her by the time she reached the bottom. Still on the second-to-bottom step, she threw her arms around his neck.

"Are you OK?" Daniel turned on his phone light again as he came behind Emily. "Did someone lock you down here?"

Milt Garrett chuckled mirthlessly. "Sorry to say, it was your friend Ryan."

"What?" Daniel and Emily asked in unison.

"Yeah," Milt began. "OK, it was last night. I was sitting with your friends in the dining room. Most of the other guests had long ago checked out. You two were on the road, and Brandon and his girl were holed up in their room. Stacey was at the front desk." He paused and looked directly at Emily. "I'm not sure why. Good kid, eh? Anyway, the electricity went out for a longer time than usual, and the generator hadn't kicked in. I said I was going to the basement to check on it."

Milt had been gazing upward in thought as he recalled the incidents; now he met Daniel's eyes. "That's when your friend Ryan said he'd come with me to help. Hey, I thought it would be nice to have an extra hand, and I took him up on it. When we got to the basement, he let me go first. Then he shut the door. I thought that was odd, so I turned around and tried the doorknob. It was stuck."

"That's crazy," Daniel interjected.

"I know."

Emily jumped in. "He put a wooden board up against the knob, keeping you from being able to leave."

Milt grunted his frustration. "I called out, and when the guy didn't respond, I pounded on the door. It took me about five long minutes to realize that he had done whatever he had done on purpose."

"What were you thinking?" Emily asked. "What did you do?"

Milt let out a hearty laugh this time. "I was thinking that I'd better get that generator working in order to turn on a light down here. So I did." He beamed triumphantly and then looked around and realized that they were again mostly in the dark. Daniel's phone light had begun to flicker.

"Young man, shine what's left of that light over there." Milt pointed to the generator and then walked to it, picked up the wrench on top of the box, and banged the side of the generator with the wrench. The lights sprung on, and everyone blinked.

"Anyway," Milt went on, "between banging on that generator and banging on the door every couple of hours or so, I figured I'd get found eventually. There's no cell service down here, but there is a cot in that corner"—he gestured in one direction to an army cot with a red sleeping bag thrown on it—"and a toilet and sink over there"—he gestured to the other side where, yes, a stark white toilet and sink stood. "Hey, I was fine. I even had a package of beef jerky and a jar of applesauce down here, so I was set."

Emily stepped down to meet Milt by the generator and hugged him again, and the older man smiled over her shoulder to Daniel. "This one is just the best, isn't she?" he asked.

"She sure is," Daniel confirmed.

Emily's face warmed. Then she shook her head.

Daniel leaned over to whisper in her ear. That's your 'time to move on and figure stuff out' head shake. I know you way better than you think."

Emily grinned sheepishly and moved away from the temptation that was Daniel. But then she frowned. "OK, now we have to find Ryan. What is he up to?" Her voice dropped. "Is he dangerous?"

Milt chuckled again. "I doubt it. He didn't hurt me, just locked me away. I figure he's looking for a safe or for something he can steal. I'm not that worried. I'm just really mad at being stuck down here all night."

"Stacey did say your office was locked," Emily remembered. "Maybe he's in there."

Milt started up the stairs. "Let's go then." He curled up his arm in the universal sign for "follow me."

"Are you sure it's safe?" Emily asked nervously as she brought up the rear.

Daniel scoffed. "He's a financial advisor!" he said, as if that told them everything. "And he doesn't even work out!"

Emily and Milt both laughed, as Daniel's comment had diffused the tension. When they reached the office, however, Daniel moved all three of them to the side of the door.

"Emily, do you have cell service?" Daniel asked quietly.

Emily pulled her phone out of her pocket, glanced at it, and nodded.

"Call 9-1-1 before we get in over our heads."

Emily dialed, quickly gave the information to the dispatcher, and hung up. She looked up expectantly at Daniel. He just bobbed his head once and reached across the door jamb to knock.

They heard shuffling and then quiet. Daniel knocked again, "Come on, Ryan. We know you're in there. What the heck are you doing?"

No response.

Milt moved in front of Daniel and quickly inserted his key into the doorknob. "This is silly," Milt huffed. "I want him out of my office."

## CHAPTER THIRTY-THREE

Milt barreled through the door, with Daniel and Emily right behind him. They each stopped almost immediately, nearly knocking the others over in a Keystone Cops jumble.

The three of them froze in place as they surveyed the room.

"Whoa," Daniel finally said. Nearly all of the floorboards had been torn up. Chunks and slivers of dark wood littered the ground as if dozens of tiny explosions had been set off. Ryan couldn't be easily seen on first glance, but Daniel was sure he was simply crouched down behind the desk in the center of the room. In fact, Daniel leaned sideways and could see a set of jean-clad shins.

"We know you're behind the desk," Daniel announced. "Just come out. What are you doing?"

Ryan stood up slowly from where he had been hiding. A crowbar hung limply from his right arm. Emily sucked in a loud breath, but Ryan looked down at the tool and quickly dropped it onto the desk.

"Oh, this isn't a weapon or anything." Ryan was shaking his head vigorously. "I was just digging up the floor."

"We see that!" Milt gestured around the room with both hands and then moved rather menacingly toward Ryan. Daniel gently put out an arm to halt Milt.

"I was looking for the treasure!" Ryan moaned. "It has to be in here."

"Treasure?" Milt echoed.

"From Grace Kelly."

Milt shook his head slowly in disbelief. "Oh, for heaven's sake. You're a grown man. That is an urban legend. And already proven false." He pointed around the room once again. "As you've discovered, there is nothing under these floorboards except more wood!"

"But ..." .

"Ryan, you are one pathetic dude." Daniel grabbed his co-worker's arm. "We already called the police; they're on their way."

Ryan yanked his arm from Daniel's hand but didn't try to flee. "Let me go," Ryan spit out angrily.

"You didn't just trash the place," Daniel said, just as angrily. "You kidnapped a man."

Ryan scoffed. "He was fine. No harm, no foul."

"Yes, foul!" Milt shouted. He jammed his hands into his back pockets, and Daniel could tell that the older man was resisting the urge to give Ryan a solid shove. Daniel was resisting the same urge.

"Mr. Garrett could have gotten hurt down there or not had any food or water," Emily said. Although Emily wasn't shouting, her voice was strong and firm, and she pointed her index finger at him. "You need to think about the consequences of your actions."

Ryan sneered at Emily. "Shut up."

This time, Daniel didn't resist. He elbowed Ryan in the side—hard. "Whoops, sorry," Daniel said. But he wasn't.

By Monday, the roads were clear, and Daniel and his other two work friends were ready to head home. Officer Sisko had called the night before to tell everyone that the lead detective was asking all the inn guests to stay a bit longer. He intended to stop by to make sure he had gotten all the information related to the crimes and to give the group any updates he was allowed to disclose.

Emily and Suzie had planned to meet the men in the lobby at 10 a.m., but Daniel knocked on the women's room a few minutes before 10. Suzie answered and let him in. She moved past Daniel in the open door and said that she had to go check on something. He smiled a grateful thanks to Emily's friend.

As soon as the door closed, Daniel walked to the middle of the room and hugged Emily. It was a light, one-armed hug, due to his still very sore ribs. Emily gently squeezed back, and Daniel breathed in her soft, flowery perfume.

"Weird weekend," Emily stated as she pulled back. She was wearing a black turtleneck under a navy-blue cable-knit sweater. The black set off her pale skin, pink cheeks, and blonde hair.

Daniel looked at her and sighed. Then he laughed. "You sure know how to show a guy a dangerous time!" He eased himself to sit on one of the beds, and he pulled Emily beside him so that she was propped against his uninjured ribs. "You know, I wouldn't have changed one moment!"

"I definitely would have cut out a couple of hours in the ditch," Emily observed. Then she beamed at him, her blue eyes seeming to sparkle like star sapphires.

"You're beautiful," Daniel said with no pretense or plan.

"You're not too bad yourself, *Danny*." Emily purposely emphasized his childhood nickname. "You know, on the slopes, you said you liked me and ..."

"I do."

"Well, I've liked you since I was 5." Emily touched his cheek. "I'm just glad you're finally catching up!" She smiled at him and then reclined again against his side. He gingerly brought his arm up to drape it around her shoulders. She rested her hand on his knee and sighed.

"So now what?" he asked.

"Not sure."

They sat quietly for several minutes, not looking at each other, but Daniel let himself enjoy just being where he was.

"Emmy?"

Emily twisted slightly to regard him, her eyebrows raised questioningly as she waited for him to continue.

"Are you OK with a relationship with me even though I'm not as Christian as you?"

Emily chuckled and squeezed his knee. "I'm not entirely sure that there are degrees of being Christian." She tapped her forehead and furrowed her brow slightly as she searched for a piece of information in memory. "Frederick Buechner said something like this: '"Lord, I believe; help my unbelief" is the best any of us can do really, but thank God it is enough.'" Emily took a deep breath. "We're all on different faith journeys, and God is with each of us along the way."

"I still …" Daniel let his words hang there. He wasn't sure how to finish.

"I know," Emily said. "You still don't know why God doesn't hit your brother over the head and get him out of that cult. Believe me, I get it and I wish the same thing. We just keep loving Matthew and praying for him. Let God do the rest."

"It's not easy."

Emily laughed again and kissed his cheek. "Which just gets us back to 'Lord, I believe; help my unbelief!'"

"I'm starting to believe one thing, though. I believe that God is supporting this." He waved his free hand back and forth between himself and Emily. "It feels … right."

This time, Emily kissed him on the lips, and Daniel responded. Her lips were soft and warm and promising. When they broke the kiss, he said, "That was nice."

"Mmm," Emily murmured in reply. Then she leaned her head on Daniel's shoulder. "I agree. This feels right."

She kept her head buried there for a while and then moved back to look at him again. "Well, we've handled the easy part, religion. Now we need to talk about how to manage a long-distance relationship."

Daniel smiled down into her somber face. "I think we might have already been managing that. I figure we just keep doing what we're doing—only maybe make the visits more frequent so we can do more of this." He touched her lips with two fingers.

Emily pursed those lips. "I really love it here," she admitted. "I can't see myself moving back to Philly. I mean, it's not a *Hallmark* special thing like the big city is bad or anything. But I love my job. I love my church. I love the Poconos."

"I get that," Daniel said. "For me, I like what I do, but *where* I work is not as much of a calling as where you are. I know we've only been dating for a minute and half, but ..."

Emily's sweet giggle made him break off. He seemed to be awestruck by everything she said and did. Maybe it was the painkillers, but he didn't really believe that. He kissed her gently and continued. "What I mean is, let's see where this goes. I'm a little more flexible with my living arrangements. I think I'm good at what I do, and if the time comes that we can't bear to be far apart, I'm sure I could work remotely or get a job at another firm near here."

Emily enfolded him in a hug, and Daniel winced. She quickly released him. "You are amazing," she said, and then she winked. "That means date 2 will be in Center City, right?"

# CHAPTER THIRTY-FOUR

There was a loud bang on Emily's door, and Jerry yelled, "Yo, come out of there, lovebirds. Detective Casey is here again."

Emily gave Daniel another quick peck on the cheek and rose to answer the door. Suzie was standing beside Jerry, looking sheepish. "I told him to knock *gently*." She cringed in apology.

As the four of them stepped into the hall, Jerry explained what was happening. "We're gathering in the restaurant. Apparently, the detective had gone there earlier this morning to finish asking questions of the kitchen staff. And then he called Milt down again."

When they reached the dining room, Milt was alone with the detective at a small, square table. Milt was shaking his head and holding both hands in the air in a gesture of disbelief.

Worried, Emily rushed behind him to put her hand on his shoulder, but then she heard the half-chuckle in his voice as he spoke. "I swear, there really are *no* Grace Kelly jewels. Seriously, why would she bring jewels for an overnight stay in a country inn? Yes, Sweet Fern was a bigger deal back then, but not worth storing treasure here!"

Emily watched warily as Detective Casey glanced at her standing behind Milt and then looked at the others who had gathered around the table. He was tall and muscled, with a rigid military-like bearing and matching military-like haircut. He had dark brown eyes and a straight, stern mouth. This time, however, as he assessed them, he clearly remembered who each of them were from his visit the day before. He nodded as if their presence was OK and he wasn't going to grill them, but he announced, "I need to address a personal issue with Mr. Garrett."

Milt shrugged. "OK." He turned to Emily and patted her hand, which was still on his shoulder. "I'm fine. I'll catch up with you after this."

Reluctantly, Emily stepped out into the hallway with Daniel, Jerry, and Suzie.

"What could that be about?" Suzie asked nervously.

"It is kind of weird," Jerry agreed. "What did he mean by 'personal'? Maybe Ryan stole underwear or found a secret diary."

The others laughed, but then Daniel poked his head around the doorway to peek. "He's showing Milt photos from his phone. Milt looks surprised."

"It's the underwear," Jerry declared.

As soon as Detective Casey stood, Emily and her friends spilled back into the dining room and rushed to Milt, who was still sitting at the table. The detective nodded once to the four of them as he left.

Milt now had his own phone out and was staring at it incredulously.

"Can you tell us what Detective Casey said?" Emily asked.

"Sure," Milt replied. "But it's quite a surprise. The detective texted this to me." He turned his phone for them to see. On it was a photo of a necklace laid out on a white piece of paper. Milt zoomed in to enable the rest of them to see the large, oval-shaped, faceted ruby surrounded by diamonds.

"Wow," Suzie and Emily said together.

"Cha-ching!" Jerry said almost at the same time.

"This necklace was my grandmother's," Milt explained. "Apparently Ryan found it under a bunch of papers in the bottom of the desk drawer."

"Wow!" Daniel added his own exclamation.

"In all the photos we have of my grandmom, she's wearing that necklace." Milt lowered his phone but kept looking at the photo. "She was in a nursing home the last few years of her life, and when my folks couldn't find the pendant after she died, they figured she must have sold it to pay for hospital bills. I can't believe it was in that drawer all this time. My dad's parents had given him that desk when he took over Sweet Fern decades ago."

"Under papers?" Emily asked.

"Yeah." Milt looked slightly embarrassed. "There's a bunch of old invoices for work done on the inn decades ago. I'm kind of a pack rat when it comes to documents, and I've kept them all, thinking I might someday have to consult them if we need a new roof or the like. Obviously, I haven't even had to look through them in 35 years or more!"

The rest of them began to pull up chairs from other tables around the room and crowd around the small table with Milt.

"What does this mean for you?" Daniel asked.

Milt smiled. "It means that, although there are no Grace Kelly jewels—as I've been saying—we can start getting several of the minor repairs done on the inn."

Jerry gently elbowed the older man. "No more big-box hotels like Brandon's trying to buy you out?"

"Oh, they'll keep trying," Milt replied. "But we'll have a solid balance sheet, making their offers look a lot less attractive." He rubbed his face, which made a scratching sound as his hand skimmed over his two-day-old beard. "The police will need to keep the necklace as evidence for a little bit. But the inn really isn't in any financial trouble, meaning that all of the upgrades I've suddenly begun planning in the past two minutes can wait. It just will be nice to know I'll be able to get things up to snuff the way I'd really like them."

"You know," Daniel began, "we have guys in our real estate group who could probably help you with organizing all that, if you don't have anyone already."

"Sounds good."

Emily hugged Milt, and his smiled broadened. "You're stuck with us and the inn for a while, little lady," Milt said to her.

"I wouldn't have it any other way."

Milt looked up at Daniel. "I told you she was the best."

# CHAPTER THIRTY-FIVE

By early spring, after Mr. Garrett's floor had been refinished, several other updates were under way, and the snow had finally melted completely, Daniel and Emily had gotten into a comfortable long-distance-dating routine. Daniel was a little disappointed that their schedules weren't conducive to true every-weekend visits, but their trips did amount to them seeing each other two or three times a month, with the Poconos and Philadelphia getting equal time.

It was the Poconos' turn, and Daniel was driving straight to the Deer Head Inn in Delaware Water Gap on Friday night to meet Emily for dinner after work. Emily had been talking about this for weeks. The restaurant billed itself as "the oldest continuously running jazz club in the country," and it regularly hosted top names in the world of jazz. It even had its own record label. Musicians seemed to love the atmosphere of the white clapboard home with the small and intimate interior that was paneled in dark wood. One could sleep, dine, listen to live music, or do all three. Emily and Daniel had plans to eat and then listen to a jazz pianist with a three-piece ensemble. Emily had seen the woman perform at the Deer Head several years earlier. "Mesmerizing" was the word Emily used when she told Daniel about it.

Daniel arrived right on time for their 7 p.m. reservation, and Emily was still standing on the restaurant's front porch talking to one of the owners of the venue. When he caught her eye as she walked from the parking lot, she grinned, and Daniel saw her bite her lower lip in anticipation. He marveled at how she still made his heart leap every time he saw her.

As soon as he stepped on the porch, she reached up and put both her hands into his hair to muss it.

"Hey," Daniel pretended to protest. He patted it back into place. In deference to her, he had begun to grow his hair just a little longer. He liked it when she ran her fingers through it, but he wasn't going to say that in public.

Emily gave him the once-over and rolled her eyes. "Even out of your work clothes, you still look like a *GQ* model." He had changed before he left, and now he looked down at his casual, lilac, cotton crewneck sweater and faded jeans. He shrugged.

"You just look very put together," Emily said. "I'm lucky I could find clothes that were warm but not too wintery!" She had on a red-and-white, horizontal-striped, scoop-neck shirt, which Daniel had seen before and had complimented her on. He smiled to himself, sure that she had remembered that earlier compliment.

"Ready?" the owner asked. "Are you staying for the music?

"We are," Emily said. "She's wonderful."

"She is." The owner grabbed two menus and walked them to their seats off the left of the small stage. "Is this OK?"

After they ordered—Emily had recommended the beet and goat cheese salad—they ate and chatted about the past week. They were in what Daniel's friends teased him was the "lovey-dovey" stage of their relationship, and Daniel often thought it might be OK to stay this way for a long time, no matter how much people joked about it. He knew that he looked into each Emily's eyes and smiled a lot, and he constantly reached across the table to hold her hand. That's why he was surprised when the guitarist, drummer, and upright bass player began softly playing a jazz standard as background music. This indicated that the piano player would soon move to the stage and begin entertaining them.

Daniel frowned. "Oh, I wanted to tell you something, but I guess it can wait until they take their first break."

Emily looked concerned. "Do you want to go outside and talk?"

"No, it can wait." Daniel gave her a half-smile. "It's nothing bad— just work stuff. You said she's amazing; this is what we came for."

And she *was* amazing. This woman had been playing jazz for nearly 20 years, and the ease with which she moved from one melody to the next and fluttered her way up and down the keys had the audience enthralled.

"She moves so fast," Daniel commented between two of the songs.

"And it never sounds 'wrong,'" Emily whispered back.

When the band finally took a break, Daniel once again reached for Emily's hand across the table. She felt a little nervous, although she wasn't sure why. He had said it wasn't bad, and she believed him. On the other hand, it was too soon for them to be taking huge next steps in their relationship. In addition, she had her own news to share, and she was just as anxious to see how that news would affect the two of them.

Daniel began: "Barner and Barner is moving to Scranton, and they asked me to take a managerial position there." He paused for just a moment. "I'd be way closer to you, and I really want to do it. What do you think?"

Emily's jaw dropped. She wasn't sure what she was expecting, but this wasn't it. This was good news, she thought, yet she wanted to be sure that he was sure.

"But you love the city," she said.

"But I love you more." Daniel's reply was made simply but seriously, and it induced a little shiver in Emily. He kept going: "And it's the activity of city life that I really love, not Philadelphia especially.

Scranton is a city. It doesn't have to be Philadelphia. I'm just tired of waiting sometimes weeks between seeing you."

"Me too," Emily agreed. "I do really love you, Daniel. It would be way better to see you more often. As soon as you leave on a weekend, I miss you." She wrinkled her nose. "Oh, does that sound corny?"

Daniel actually blushed, which warmed Emily all over.

"It's not corny." He lifted a shoulder. "It's kinda cool."

Emily took a deep breath. "I have news too. The Jenners are moving to San Francisco, to be closer to their daughter."

"Your neighbors who own Chloe?"

"Yeah." Emily nodded. "Remember, their daughter just had her first child last month, and they want to spend more time with the daughter and the baby. They can't take a dog where they're moving to, and they want to give Chloe to me. I can't keep a dog in my apartment, so ..." Emily sucked in air once again. "They asked if I wanted to buy their house."

"Wow." Daniel leaned back in his chair but continued to watch her face. "What do you think?"

When Emily smiled, she could tell she was beaming. "Oh, I really want to buy it! I knew I had to talk with you first. I wasn't sure how we were going to resolve this Philly-Poconos thing, so I didn't know whether or not to say yes. But if you'll just be over the mountain in Scranton ..."

"Sounds like the universe is pushing us together."

"I'm gonna put this one on God, not the universe," Emily said, and this time, her smile was more tentative. "It feels like God chose us to be together. And it makes me think of Romans 8:28."

Daniel nodded. "I agree. And you may be surprised to hear that I actually know that verse." He straightened to recite it. "'We know that all things work together for good for those who love God.'"

# EPILOGUE

## OUTER BANKS, NORTH CAROLINA

Fourteen Months Later

Emily could tell that her sister was nervous. The DJ announced Abby's name, and she stood up, holding her glass in one hand and clutching her typed-out maid-of-honor speech in the other. She glanced off to the right, looking out the huge picture windows of the family center of the United Methodist Church. Emily followed Abby's gaze. Outside, the water of the Currituck Sound shimmered and sparkled with alternating strips of blue-black and then white, reflecting the afternoon sun.

From her still-seated position, Emily reached up to touch her sister's arm and sighed happily.

Abby bit her bottom lip, and Emily smiled at the familiar family trait. Her sister took a steadying breath and looked out over the banquet floor.

"This is a special wedding for both our families," Abby began. "As many of you know, our father and Daniel's father met—sorry, Dads, for revealing this—over 30 years ago when they were freshmen in college and became fraternity brothers." Abby nodded toward the family table where both fathers—and mothers—were beaming. "That fact actually garnered my dad a few strange looks at work this week when he announced proudly: 'I'm very excited. This weekend, my daughter is marrying my brother's son!' He neglected to emphasize *frat* brother!"

The wedding guests laughed, and Emily could see Abby relax.

"I am touched to be my little sister's maid of honor," Abby continued. "She is an amazing woman, and I am very proud of her. However, when a maid of honor gets up for her speech, because she's known the bride the longest, she tells sweet and silly stories about the bride and welcomes the groom into the circle of family and friends. Of course, I'm in the unique position of having known my new brother-in-law for three years *before* I met my own sister! Our folks and Daniel's folks"— Abby glanced toward another table—"and the Kotchkas and Delanceys —we all vacationed together from the time our sister Paige was a toddler; Daniel, Aaron, and I were in diapers; and Emily wasn't even around yet!"

Once again, a titter went through the group, accompanied by several "Aww's." Abby went on to regale the wedding guests with adventures from their beach vacations. Emily giggled when her sister didn't keep back mentioning the time that four-year-old Daniel took off his bathing suit trunks on the beach and ran into the ocean naked just because he wanted to "see what it felt like." And, of course, Abby had to tell of the numerous times that Emily jockeyed to sit next to Daniel at dinner and put her arms around him—one time doing it so zealously that she actually punched Daniel in the eye trying to hug him.

"I forgot about that," Daniel chimed in. He looked at Emily. "You're forgiven."

Their brother Aaron couldn't resist commenting as well: "Even after the punch, though, she held on tight."

Abby shook her head, chuckled, and continued: "It was all about 'adventures' for us when we were kids. And now you have the ultimate adventure—the adventure of marriage." Abby looked down again at her sister and sighed. "Emily, you are full of the joy of life, and Daniel is lucky that you're sharing that joy with him." Then she turned to Daniel: "And Daniel, when we were younger, we always said that we Outer Banks kids were 'just like family.' But now, you *are* family. Welcome."

Abby smiled more broadly and raised her glass. "And all of us—family and friends—are very glad that God saw fit to let the two of you find each other again. Cheers."

After clinking glasses with Daniel, Emily leaned over and kissed her new husband on the cheek. She tasted the tears that had slipped out during her sister's toast.

Daniel returned the kiss, this time on the lips, to the delight of the guests.

Then he looked up at Abby and whispered, "Thank you." He stood up and leaned behind Emily's chair to hug his new sister-in-law.

Emily stood then, too, and joined the hug. "I love you," she said to Abby.

"I'm glad Matthew was here at the reception to hear your toast," Daniel observed quietly as the three of them leaned out of the embrace. "I only wish he would have gone to the ceremony and heard the Scriptures and the things the minister said."

"One step at a time," Abby advised as they all sat again. "I understand that it's a big coup to get him and his wife to even come to the party."

"'And now faith, hope, and love abide, these three,'" Emily said, quoting First Corinthians 13. "We have the faith and the love, for sure. Just hold on to that hope!"

Daniel looked into his bride's eyes, and she saw his own eyes brimming. "God gave me you," he said. "And through you, I found my faith again. I'll always hope."

# THANK YOU

Special thanks to all my friends and family who helped in the creation of this book, especially Barbara McGrath, Nancy Kinsman, Thea Howey, Suzanne Oliver, Kim McSweeney, Kristine Grow, Lee Wheeler, Evelyn Allen, Tara Picht, Carolyn Springer, Truman Brooks, and Joe McGinty.

And, of course, thanks to God, who gives us diverse gifts. May you use yours all for good.

If you enjoyed this book, please consider leaving an honest review on Amazon.com.

# ABOUT THE AUTHOR

Roseann McGrath Brooks is a full-time editor, part-time college writing tutor, and all-the-time believer in God and love. She has a BA in English and French and an MA in Humanities.

Roseann lives in Pennsylvania with her minister husband and thanks God every day for him, their two children, their three grand-children, and the rest of her amazingly supportive family.

Please visit her website at roseannmcgrathbrooksauthor.com

Made in the USA
Middletown, DE
18 October 2020

22103057R00111